MUSTANG in the MIST

by Ben M. Baglio

Illustrations by Ann Baum

Cover illustration by
Mary Ann Lasher

SCHOLASTIC INC.
New York Toronto London Auckland Sydney
Mexico City New Delhi Hong Kong Buenos Aires

Special thanks to Stephen Cole

ISBN-13: 978-0-439-77524-3
ISBN-10: 0-439-77524-8

Text copyright © 2005 by Working Partners Limited.
Created by Working Partners Limited, London W6 0QT.
Illustrations copyright © 2005 by Scholastic Inc.

12 11 10 9 8 7 6 5 4   7 8 9 10 11 12/0

Printed in the U.S.A.   40
First Scholastic printing, March 2006

One

"Jump a half-turn to the right and get ready with the handclaps. . . . One and two and three and *CLAP*!"

The crowd sprang sideways, more or less in time to the music. From a seat at the side of the hall, Mandy Hope grinned. Her gran and grandpa were standing in a line with two other couples, all looking dead serious as they concentrated on following the instructors' moves.

Mandy's best friend, James Hunter, leaned over to speak in her ear. "I never would have guessed your grandparents were dancers," he said. "But they're really good!"

"They are, aren't they?" Mandy agreed proudly. Gran

and Grandpa had been to a few line-dance lessons already, and had taken to it like ducks to water. Grandpa was even wearing a red-and-blue plaid shirt and a battered Stetson that Gran had found in a thrift store. Full of enthusiasm, they had invited Mandy along to a class with them at Welford Village Hall; she had persuaded James to come, too, but he had looked very relieved when they had arrived too late for the start of the class.

James looked nervously at the dance instructors, a man and a woman in their late twenties wearing plaid shirts and blue denim jeans. "I hope they don't make us dance by ourselves," he whispered. "I think I'd rather watch from the side today."

"Chicken," teased Mandy.

"Where?" joked James, pretending to look around. "We're not at Animal Ark!"

Animal Ark was the veterinary practice run by Mandy's parents in the Yorkshire village of Welford. Mandy usually hated being late for anything, but this evening she had been helping a nervous tortoiseshell cat settle into the residential unit behind the clinic. Sherpa had a bad kidney infection and needed a course of antibiotics before he could go home to his anxious owners.

"Maybe I should go back and make sure Sherpa's still OK," James suggested, wriggling uncomfortably on his chair. "We've got a lot in common — I'm feeling nervous in *my* new surroundings, too!"

"Pumping now — all start forward with the left foot," called the female dance instructor. Her name was Lisa Cooke, and she was a tall, slim woman with jet-black hair and smiling brown eyes.

"That's right, really pump those elbows," said her husband, Paul, a round-faced man with short brown hair, as he marched on the spot beside her. Like his wife, he had an American accent. He was a little shorter than Lisa, and his wide-spaced almond-shaped eyes shone with enthusiasm. "Remember, pump once with each count of the beat — but take a step every *two* counts and a clap on four!"

"*Step* and two and *step* and *clap*," chanted Lisa. She flipped her long hair over her shoulder and nodded her head. "OK, now grapevine to the left, everybody!"

Mandy thought it sounded like a cross between a math lesson and biology.

"What are you two doing, sitting there?" a voice demanded suddenly.

Mandy looked up to see Paul Cooke smiling in their direction, his blue eyes twinkling. "Come and join in!"

"We can't!" James gulped, turning bright red.

Mandy nodded. "We got here too late. We haven't even paid —"

"No one sits through one of our lessons," Paul said firmly. "They dance! So come on. Consider it a special offer."

"Yeah, come on, you two!" called Grandpa Hope. "It's fun!"

"I'd love to!" Mandy admitted, jumping to her feet.

"But we don't know what to do!" James protested.

"Just watch what everyone else is doing and listen to us," said Paul. "You'll pick it up." He turned back to face the rest of the class. "Now, next eight counts, jump a quarter-turn to the left and a half-turn to the right . . ."

Mandy and James joined the shortest of the four lines and tried to fall into step with the others. Putting their feet in the right places, clapping their hands, *and* keeping in time to the music was trickier than it looked! Luckily, there were several other beginners in Mandy's line. The better dancers were at the front, so the less experienced students behind could copy them.

"So this is what they meant by a grapevine," Mandy gasped, swinging her arms and crisscrossing her feet.

"My legs keep getting tangled up," puffed James. "I feel like a sick pigeon, flapping around like this!"

"Good thing you're coming back to Animal Ark with me for dinner." Mandy grinned. A new song came on, and she recognized it with delight. "Hey, it's 'Saddles and Spurs' by the Cowboys! They're my favorite band right now."

"I saw them on TV last night," said James, jumping a three-quarter-turn. "I used to think they were an American band, but they're British, aren't they?"

Mandy nodded breathlessly. "This song always makes me want to dance — but I never thought I'd be dancing like *this*!"

"Well done," called Lisa as the song came to an end. "Thank you, everybody, that's it for today. Don't forget, there is no class next Friday. But we will be holding a class in Walton on Wednesday night."

"It's going to be good, too!" Paul added temptingly. "We'll be introducing some pigeon-toed moves, with knee pops and hip bumps."

"Sounds like a doctor should be on hand!" Grandpa Hope chuckled, joining Mandy and James. "Phew, I'm out of breath after all that."

"Did you have fun?" asked Gran.

Mandy nodded. "It was great!"

"I think I'll stick to watching next time," said James. "The person in front of me kept stepping on my toes!"

"Well, I definitely want to do a whole class," Mandy said decidedly. "Too bad there won't be one next Friday." She tucked her hair behind her ears, feeling rather disheveled. "Come on, James. We should thank Paul and Lisa for giving us a free sample!"

"I guess." James sighed, rubbing his shins.

"Hey!" Paul beamed as they approached. "You two are naturals! Will you come again?"

"Maybe," James said hesitantly. "As long as there aren't any more animal emergencies!"

"Is that why you missed the beginning?" Lisa asked. "I hope it wasn't anything serious."

"Actually, my parents are vets, and we have a lot of animals staying at the clinic right now," Mandy explained.

Lisa raised her eyebrows. "Your folks wouldn't own Animal Ark, would they?"

"That's right," Mandy said. "I'm Mandy Hope, and this is James Hunter. He lives in Welford, too."

Lisa turned to Paul. "We've got to get in touch with Animal Ark this week. We need a good veterinarian, and we've heard great things about the Hopes."

"Good idea," Paul agreed.

Just then a group of people came up to ask for more details about the Wednesday night classes. Lisa gave a quick wave to Mandy and mouthed, "See you soon."

Mandy and James walked over to join Gran and Grandpa Hope by the door. "What would line-dance instructors want with a vet?" Mandy wondered aloud.

James grinned. "Maybe it's got something to do with those pigeon toes they mentioned."

Gran and Grandpa dropped Mandy, James, and their bicycles back at Animal Ark. It was almost eight o'clock.

"Perfect timing!" said Mandy's mother, Dr. Emily Hope, as they came into the kitchen. She had just finished slicing a large loaf of bread. "Adam!" she called. "We're ready for dinner."

Dr. Adam Hope came into the kitchen and smiled. "Hey, you two. Hope you weren't too late for class."

"I almost wish we'd been a little later," said James. "My legs still ache!"

"It was great," Mandy said firmly. "But how's Sherpa doing?"

"He was asleep when I looked in on him a few minutes ago," her dad told her. "You really helped settle him in by sitting with him before. He hasn't eaten yet, so later on you can try to get some food in him."

"But for now, eat your own dinner," said Dr. Emily, handing out plates. "So, you managed to join in with some of the class, huh?"

Mandy nodded. "Gran was right about Paul and Lisa Cooke, they're both really good teachers."

"Too bad they couldn't teach the person in front of me not to crush my feet!" James grumbled.

"It's nice that they've decided to get involved with the community like this," said Dr. Emily. "They've only been here a few weeks, but already their classes are the talk of Welford. They're from Texas, aren't they?"

"I think that's what Gran said," Mandy agreed, pouring glasses of lemonade for herself and James. "San Antonio."

"Seems a long way to come to teach line dancing," said James through a mouthful of bread.

Dr. Adam nodded. "According to Mrs. McFarlane in the post office, they've moved into Bottom Farm. I wonder what they'll do with it. The Yorkshire Dales must be very different from Texas."

"Well, you'll be able to ask them soon," said Mandy, helping herself to another slice of bread. "Lisa said they needed to call you this week, so I guess they have animals."

"Just as long as *they* don't line dance, too." Dr. Adam laughed. "Imagine the problems we'd have trying to examine them!"

After they'd helped clear away the food and dishes, Mandy and James took a saucer of mashed tuna to Sherpa's cage in the residential unit. The cat's green eyes gleamed in the dark for a moment before the lights flickered on.

"Dinnertime, Sherpa," Mandy murmured, opening the cage and sliding the plate underneath his tiny pink nose. Then she went back to stand by James at the door.

"I really hope he eats something," she whispered. Sometimes animals felt so nervous about being in a strange place that they lost their appetite, which didn't help their recovery.

Suddenly, Sherpa's whiskers twitched and he lifted his head, his triangular ears pointing straight up. Mandy squeezed James's arm excitedly as the cat began nibbling at some of the tuna, then started lapping up the chunks with more enthusiasm. He ate almost the whole portion before resting his head on his bedding again, his pink tongue flicking over his lips.

"He did really well," Mandy said happily as she went over to remove the plate. "He needs to keep his strength up while the antibiotics do their work."

"I'd better head home, now that we've all eaten," said James. "There's important thinking to be done."

Mandy raised her eyebrows. "Oh, yeah?"

"About what to do during spring break, of course," James reminded her. "Two weeks with no school!"

"If the weather's nice, we could go for a hike in the fields," Mandy suggested.

"Great idea," said James. "Especially if we take a picnic. Where could we go?"

Mandy thought for a moment. "How about up to Axwith Tor?"

"That's a long hike," James said cautiously.

"We don't have to walk all the way from here. Dad has to drop off some deworming medication at High Cross Farm tomorrow morning," Mandy said. "We can go with him and leave from Lydia's. It's not as far from there."

"And from Axwith Tor, we'll get a good view into the next valley." James grinned. "You might even be able to spot Bottom Farm! That was why you suggested it, wasn't it?"

"Maybe," Mandy admitted. "Your dad's got some binoculars, doesn't he? Can you borrow them?"

"Sure," said James. "I'll ask him as soon as I get home."

Mandy walked with him to the front door. "I'll give you a call before we leave in the morning," she promised.

As the lights on James's bike dwindled into the dark, chilly night, Mandy shut the door. Then, remembering what she'd learned in the dance class, she spun on her heel in a half-turn and grapevined nimbly up the stairs and across the landing to her bedroom. Her legs were tingling with the evening's exercise, and she decided to get into her pajamas and go to bed early. The sooner she went to bed, the sooner she and James might discover which mystery animals lived at the Cookes' new home!

Mandy and her dad left for High Cross Farm at nine o'clock the next morning and picked up James along the way. Axwith Tor was a rocky hilltop peak, formed when wind and rain wore away the soil to expose the topmost layers of rock. The tor loomed over the fields that stretched away beneath it, folding into steep-sided valleys where glittering silver rivers ran. Thin trails of mist curled around the hills, streaking the dark green heather like huge cobwebs.

"It's a beautiful morning," Mandy remarked.

"A little chilly for a picnic, though," said Dr. Adam. "Did you pack extra clothes?"

Mandy patted her backpack. "And a poncho."

James pulled out a small, black case from his own bag. "I've got my dad's binoculars," he said. "And my cell phone. We're all set!"

"Are you sure of your route?" asked Dr. Adam.

"We'll take the main trail there and back," Mandy told him. "But I brought a map, so if we feel like exploring, we can still find our way back."

Her dad steered the Land Rover onto the rutted track

that wound to High Cross Farm and stopped beside a clearing that led to the tor trail. "I've got a few places to visit this morning," he said, "but I'll be back here at one-thirty to pick you up. Will that be enough time for your hike?"

"Sounds perfect," said Mandy. "We'll meet you at the farm. That way we'll be able to visit Lydia's goats, too."

She and James got out of the Land Rover and waved Dr. Adam off as he continued down the road.

"Hey, maybe we should try grapevining our way up to the tor!" Mandy suggested, climbing over a short stone wall and walking a couple of steps on the sheep-cropped grass.

James made a face. "Not in hiking boots!"

The trail led them through sunshine and shadow as it climbed steeply toward the tor. After a while they stopped to enjoy the view and drink some water from the bottle in Mandy's backpack. Lydia's farm was spread out below them like a toy farm. The goats looked like tiny cotton balls in the field, and cars appeared miniature rolling along the road. To the west lay Welford and, just before the village, through a haze of mist, Mandy picked out Sam Western's farm, Upper Welford Hall.

As they set off again, the sun vanished behind a cloud. Mandy tried out a few line-dance steps to warm herself up, hoping the weather would stay nice. But before long, dark clouds rolled across the sky, and the craggy peak above them disappeared in a heavy cloak of mist.

"So much for the sunny day." James sighed as they put on their ponchos. "We won't be able to see a thing through the binoculars if this keeps up."

The higher they hiked, the worse the weather became. Soon they were pulling up their hoods against a steady, persistent drizzle. Mandy looked around uneasily as the mist thickened, turning the landscape into a featureless gray blur. It was unusually quiet, with not even the sound of birdsong to suggest there was anything else alive on the moor. With a shiver, Mandy walked faster, and almost stumbled as she strayed off the trail.

They climbed on in silence until the ground began to level out under their feet. "We must be near the tor," Mandy puffed.

"Let's look for shelter," said James. Their jeans were soaked and clung to their skin, and the exposed granite was slippery with rain. But at last they found a big, overhanging rock and huddled beneath it.

"What a drag!" James declared.

Mandy could hear his teeth chattering. "Let's have lunch," she suggested. "We'll need plenty of energy for the hike back down, and it will make our backpacks lighter."

"Maybe the weather will clear up by then," said James as he munched miserably on a cheese sandwich.

"Can I borrow your phone?" Mandy asked when she'd finished her apple. "I should call Dad and tell him we reached the tor in one piece."

James pulled the phone from his bag and squinted at the display. "No signal!" he groaned.

His words echoed spookily off the rock. Mandy peered out, seeing nothing but dense gray mist. Even the tor was barely visible, little more than a dark gray shadow at the top of the hill. She shuddered at the thought of getting lost up here.

"We've got to make sure we stick to the trail on our way down," she said, crawling out from under the rocky ledge and standing up. But as she bent down to pick up her backpack, her muddy boot slipped. With a gasp, Mandy fell backward, hitting her head on the edge of the overhanging rock. She landed heavily on the ground and lay still for a few moments, waiting for her head to stop spinning.

"Mandy!" James cried, his voice strangely deadened by the thick mist. "Are you all right?"

She sat up and gingerly felt the back of her head. "I bumped my head," she said. "But I think I'm OK."

James shuffled out from the little cave and stood beside her. "Come on, let me help you up."

But when Mandy got to her feet, she suddenly felt dizzy, and she staggered, grabbing hold of James to stop herself from falling down again. "Sorry!"

"Don't worry," he panted, flailing his arms to get his balance. "Are you all right to walk?"

She nodded, wincing as her head started to ache. "I think so."

"We should head back down and see if we can get a signal on the phone," said James. "Then we can call your dad to come and get us."

"Which way is the path?"

"I'm not sure," James admitted. "We spun around when we stood up. I think it's this way."

They set off, holding on to each other for support. Mandy's head was throbbing, and she longed to see the comforting sight of the trail ahead. But there was just slick, solid granite under their feet, and the gray blanket of mist all around.

At last, the stone gave way to peaty grass and a path stretched ahead of them down the hill, the beaten earth trail swallowed up quickly by the mist.

Mandy took a couple of uncertain steps. "It seems narrower than the path we took coming up."

James peered at his compass. "I don't think it's right, either. Should we keep looking?"

Mandy felt a wave of dizziness come over her. "No, I

think we should take it," she said, pushing her wet bangs out of her eyes. "Even if it's not the right path, I know most of the farmers around here. If we go down into a valley, we're bound to find someone we can ask to help us get back to High Cross."

They followed the winding path down the hillside. The valley below was full of mist, so Mandy couldn't tell where they were. She kept straining to see any signs of a farmhouse or a cottage, her head aching more with every step.

"Can we rest for a minute?" she asked James, bending over and putting her hands on her knees.

"Of course," he said. Then he frowned. "What's that noise?"

Mandy listened. It was quiet for a moment. Then, to her amazement, she could hear thundering hooves coming up the hill toward them, together with a curious whooping noise.

Suddenly, to her complete astonishment, a cowboy galloped out of the mist on a beautiful buckskin horse!

Two

Mandy decided she must have banged her head harder than she thought. It was like a dream. The rider was wearing a white Stetson hat and fringed leather chaps, like someone out of a Western film. The horse was not particularly tall, maybe fifteen hands, but its slender frame looked strong and well muscled. The bridle was made of fancy leather, doubled and stitched with beautiful silver stars, while the saddle was cherry-red, larger and more rugged than any Mandy had seen before, and secured by a wide leather breast collar. The horse's legs, muzzle, and ear tips were glossy black to match its mane and tail, while its coat was a gorgeous creamy fawn color, like the palest shade of wheat.

"Whoa, there!" cried the rider, pulling the reins. The horse slithered to a stop in the space of a single stride, and Mandy suddenly realized that the cowboy was a cow*girl*.

"It's Lisa Cooke!" James exclaimed at the same moment.

"Hey, guys!" said Lisa, sounding surprised. "I didn't expect to find you up here! This isn't the greatest weather for a hike up the tor."

"The mist caught us by surprise," James admitted.

"Us, too," said Lisa.

Mandy opened her mouth to ask Lisa if she knew where the path led, but a wave of dizziness swept over her and she shut it again, reaching out to put her hand on the nearest boulder to keep herself upright.

Lisa looked concerned. "Are you OK?"

"She slipped and hit her head," explained James.

"I'd better take a look." Lisa swung herself down to the ground, looped the reins over the horse's head, and dropped the ends on the ground. She fished a first-aid kit out of one of the leather saddlebags and walked over to Mandy. Her horse watched her with his ears pricked but didn't move a muscle, even though he wasn't hitched to anything.

As Lisa opened the first-aid kit, Mandy heard a second set of galloping hooves tearing over the fields in the distance. The buckskin horse turned his head to look but didn't try to follow.

"So it's horses!" Mandy guessed, smiling weakly. "You have horses that you want my mom and dad to see!"

"Yep!" said Lisa with a grin. "That's Paul you hear, giving China some exercise! Now, let me look at that head of yours." She doused a cotton ball in antiseptic and wiped it gently over the bump on the back of Mandy's head.

Trying not to flinch away, Mandy studied the horse. "He's beautiful," she said. "What's his name?"

"Cougar. He's pure mustang," Lisa said, putting away the cotton balls. "How does your head feel now?"

Mandy nodded carefully. "Better, thank you. Lucky for us you were passing by!"

"It's Cougar's first trip out in the fields," said Lisa. "We picked him up from the Manchester airport a couple of days ago, and figured he could use some exercise."

"Did he come over from America?" asked James.

"He's the last of our horses to arrive," Lisa confirmed, and Mandy felt a thrill of excitement that somewhere in the mist was a whole bunch of gorgeous horses that had come all the way from the United States!

She went over to take a closer look at Cougar, making

sure to approach him in full view so he wasn't surprised. As she looked into the mustang's dark, curious eyes, she almost forgot the pain in her head. He looked so intelligent and calm that it was hard to imagine he was thousands of miles from home, in a damp gray mist in a Yorkshire field. Mandy pressed her hand against his warm, damp neck, and to her delight, Cougar blew softly down his nose at her.

Lisa smiled. "I can see you get along with horses," she commented.

"Mandy's incredible with all animals," James said loyally.

"I never met a mustang before," Mandy admitted. "How did you train Cougar to stand so still without tying him up?" She was amazed that the horse still hadn't shifted so much as a hoof.

"It's called a drop-halt," Lisa explained. "When I loop the reins over his head so that they hang down to the ground, he knows he has to stand still. It's a trick we use with all the horses."

"How many horses do you have?" Mandy asked.

"About eleven," said Lisa.

Mandy and James looked at each other in surprise. "Eleven!" they said in unison.

Lisa grinned. "Actually, for a full-blown Western riding center it's not so many."

"A Western riding center?" Mandy echoed excitedly. "Here in Welford? That sounds too good to be true!"

"Well, they say seeing is believing," said Lisa. "Why don't you come back to the ranch and take a look for yourselves? You could call your parents from there and have them come get you."

Mandy smiled at James and spoke for them both. "We'd love to!"

"Good. Mandy, you can ride with me on Cougar. And as for you, James . . ." Lisa tipped her head to one side as the sound of hooves grew louder. "Hey, Paul! Over here!"

Another cowboy rode out of the mist, this time on a powerful, black-and-white mare with thick, muscular shoulders and a short neck. Paul Cooke looked very different from when he had been leading the line-dance class. He was dressed in black tasseled suede and there were spurs on his calf-length leather boots. His face looked tanned and handsome under the broad brim of his Stetson, which was black to match his suede jacket.

"Howdy, pardners!" he called in an exaggerated American accent.

"They're not tourists, Paul." Lisa pretended to scold him. "It's Mandy and James, from the line-dance class!"

"So it is," Paul declared, recognizing them and waving to them both. "A little far off the beaten track, aren't you?"

"We fell off it!" James told him.

Lisa Cooke explained to her husband what had happened. Paul nodded sympathetically. "We'd better get you back down to the ranch," he agreed. He shifted forward in the saddle and twisted around to pat the space behind him. "Hop aboard!" he said to James.

"You won't go too fast, will you?" James said warily.

"She's very steady," Paul assured him, "and we'll take it nice and slow." He bent down to grasp James's hand and heaved him onto China's broad, checkerboard-colored back.

"Come on, Mandy," said Lisa, springing easily back into Cougar's saddle. "Can you manage to climb on?"

"I think so." Mandy stood on top of the boulder and swung herself up behind Lisa. A stretch of thick blanket stuck out from underneath the saddle, and Mandy wriggled onto the edge, holding on to Lisa's waist.

"All secure there?" Lisa checked. "Don't worry, it's a lot less misty farther down."

Cougar set off, his bit jangling as he picked his way down the trail. China fell in behind them, matching Cougar's pace perfectly.

"They're not about to break into a line-dance routine, are they?" James joked.

"They're well-trained, but not *that* well-trained!" replied Paul. "Line dancing's just a hobby we got into back in Texas, to make sure we didn't spend *every* moment of our time working on the ranch! We've never been tempted to combine it with our horses."

"If you had a ranch and all these horses in Texas," Mandy said, holding on more tightly to Lisa's waist as the trail started to slope steeply, "what made you move all the way over here? It must be very different from the States!"

"It sure is," Lisa agreed. "But I'm actually one-quarter English. My grandpa owned Bottom Farm, and we came here on vacation every summer. When he passed away last year, he left the farm to me, knowing how much I loved it."

"We did a lot of thinking before we moved here," Paul explained, encouraging China to walk alongside now that the trail was leveling out. "But in the end, we both felt like we wanted a new challenge."

"Plus I wanted to keep the farm in the family," Lisa added. "And since Paul's got family over here, too, and a few business contacts . . ."

"We decided to try it over here, along with all our favorite horses!" said Paul. "The horizon may be a little smaller over here, but the countryside is just as beautiful as the Texan plains — even in the mist!"

"It's still a really big decision," Mandy said admiringly.

Lisa shrugged. "I guess it's the Old West spirit, but coming the other way across the Atlantic!" She ran her hand down Cougar's dark glossy mane. "Which makes this fella a four-legged pioneer!"

James frowned. "Isn't a mustang a kind of sports car, or an old warplane?"

"They were named after the horse," Paul corrected him. "*Mustang* is an old word, from the Mexican Spanish *mestengo*. Roughly translated, it means 'stray' or 'ownerless.' It was the name given to all horses running wild in North America a couple of centuries ago, but now it's developed into a very specific breed." He paused to let China find her way around some loose rocks on the path. "Wild horses mated with domesticated breeds such as Morgans and quarter horses when the cowboys turned them out to forage in the winter months, and that created a type of horse that was finer in build and a little shorter-legged than the quarter horses, with the Morgan's good-looking features. But Cougar's very special because he's one hundred percent pure mustang."

"And one hundred percent amazing," Mandy murmured.

"Did you have to leave the horses in quarantine for ages?" James asked.

Paul shook his head. "Horses can't contract rabies,

which is the main reason for leaving animals in quarantine. Besides, they all have their own passports and medical records. Travel for them is really straightforward."

To Mandy's relief, the path led them out of the mist and a patch of sunlight broke through the clouds, casting a watery beam of light into the valley. Ahead of them, about halfway down the side of the hill, Mandy could make out a cluster of buildings.

"Is that Bottom Farm?" she asked, pointing.

Lisa glanced over her shoulder and grinned. "Well, it used to be." She reined Cougar to a halt next to a wooden gate and jumped down to the ground, swinging her right leg over Cougar's neck in front of the saddle because Mandy was sitting behind. She opened the gate and nodded to Mandy. "You can take him down the trail to the yard."

"Really?" Mandy said in astonishment. "I've never ridden Western style before!"

"You'll be fine," Lisa promised. "Just keep your reins loose and don't try to kick. Cougar knows where to go."

Mandy wriggled forward until she was sitting in the saddle and then slid her feet into the stirrups. Her legs were not much shorter than Lisa's, but the stirrup leathers seemed very long, and her knees were hardly bent. The saddle was very deep and comfortable, and it

seemed quite natural to sit up straight with her legs
hanging lightly on either side. She held the reins in both
hands but kept them loose enough for Cougar to stretch
his head.

"Walk on, boy," she said, and with a toss of his head,
the mustang stepped through the gate and down the
stony trail. It curved down the hill between high stone
walls studded with ferns and little trees clinging on
with their twisted exposed roots. Mandy sat back and
enjoyed Cougar's steady pace, letting it rock her gently
in the saddle. If this was Western riding, then she loved
it! She heard Paul and James following her on China,
the mare's hooves ringing more loudly on the stones
than Cougar's delicate footsteps. Lisa brought up the
rear on foot, her tan-colored boots making no sound
at all.

Suddenly, the trail opened into a farmyard. Mandy
had only visited Bottom Farm once before with her dad,
several years ago, so she barely recognized it. But even
so, she could tell it had changed a lot! Dominating the
farmyard was a large, American-style horse barn. The
natural stone walls of the old barn had been scrubbed
clean, and the dark slate tiles were in perfect condition.
Next to the horse barn, forming another side of the yard,
was the farmhouse, painted white, with a sagging tile
roof. A row of low cowsheds made up the third side of

the yard; their walls were rough and covered in lichens, but new doors had been fitted, looking brilliant white against the stone. A wooden sign was propped up against the wall of the nearest shed, as if it was waiting to be nailed in place. Curly black lettering spelled out HART'S LEAP RANCH, and the sign was topped with a beautifully carved deer poised in mid-leap.

"Welcome to the homestead," Paul declared. "We'll have that sign up by the road when we open to the public in three weeks' time!"

"It's really eye-catching!" enthused James. "The only other Western thing around here is *Sam* Western at Upper Welford Hall!"

They all laughed. Lisa came over and looked up at Mandy. "Is that head of yours OK?"

Mandy nodded.

"Then once we've called your folks, would you and James like a guided tour?"

Mandy looked across at James, who was already nodding so hard his glasses threatened to fall off. She grinned and turned back to Lisa. "You bet we would!"

"Come on, then," she said, helping Mandy down. "We'll leave the horses with Paul, and go make sure your dad doesn't worry."

Before she followed Lisa and James into the farmhouse, Mandy stopped to thank Cougar for her first ever

Western saddle ride. Even though it had been his first outing in the Yorkshire countryside, he had looked after her as carefully as if he had known she was new to Western riding.

"See you soon," she murmured, stroking his black muzzle. It felt warm and damp from raindrops, and Mandy knew she was already smitten with the beautiful mustang who was so far from home.

Three

"I'm so sorry we kept you waiting, Dad," said Mandy, cradling the phone in the Cookes' farmhouse kitchen.

"We did try to call but there was no signal," added James, loud enough for Dr. Adam to hear. He was sitting beside Mandy at the pine dining table, hungrily eyeing the mugs of hot chocolate with marshmallows, and huge, homemade muffins that Lisa had brought out. Clearly, Lisa was determined to feel at home, even in misty Yorkshire.

"Sounds like you've had quite an adventure." Dr. Adam's voice crackled in Mandy's ear. He sounded very

31

relieved to hear from her, after waiting at High Cross Farm for fifteen minutes. "But the important thing is that you're both all right."

"We certainly are!" Mandy sipped some hot chocolate and smiled across at Lisa Cooke. "We're being very well taken care of, and my head's much better."

"Good," said Dr. Adam. "Unfortunately, I can't pick you up right away. I was due at Sam Western's farm five minutes ago. Can you hang out there a little while?"

"Uh . . ." Mandy hesitated, unsure.

Lisa understood and smiled. "Why don't you two stay here for the afternoon? Paul and I can drop you and James off on our way to Walton — we're giving another class there this evening."

"Did you catch that, Dad?" Mandy asked excitedly.

"That's very generous of Lisa," he told her. "I'll call James's parents and let them know. Thank Paul and Lisa for me, and tell them I'm looking forward to seeing all their horses."

"So am I." Mandy grinned. "Bye, Dad!"

"All set?" asked Lisa.

Mandy nodded. "I hope we won't be in your way."

"Not at all." Lisa smiled. "In fact, if you're feeling up to it, we could really use a hand! We were hoping to put the horses out for the first time this afternoon, but we need to finish fixing up the fences in the paddocks."

"I'd love to help," declared James. "But I don't think you should do any hammering, Mandy, with your sore head."

"Well, I can help put out the horses," Mandy offered.

"Two willing volunteers," said Lisa. "What a treat!"

When Mandy and James went back outside, it was just past two o'clock. The mist had cleared, except for a few cobwebby drifts clinging to the top of the tor, and the sun was shining from the pale blue sky. A few brave daffodils bobbed in the breeze, brightening the flower bed that ran the length of the farmhouse.

Lisa buckled Paul's chunky leather tool belt around her waist and passed a weighty hammer to James. "Thanks for helping," she told him. "The two of us will finish off the fencing in no time."

"As for us, Mandy," said Paul, "we need to get the horses booted up before we turn them out."

"Booted up?" Mandy echoed.

"Sure — brushing boots." He led the way over to the barn. "The horses aren't used to the steep, rocky ground yet, so we use padded waterproof boots to protect their fetlocks." He caught Mandy looking puzzled, and quickly went on, "Don't worry, they're not like rain boots for people. They wrap around the horse's leg between the knee and the fetlock, which is that bony part just above the hoof, and are held together with Velcro."

He heaved open the double doors at one end of the barn to reveal a wide central aisle made from spotless cream-colored concrete. To the left was a cluttered tack room, with a warm scent of oil and leather. On the right was an open space, like a stable with no walls and no straw on the floor. Mandy guessed this was where the horses were groomed — the large brass ring set into the concrete wall must be for tying them up.

There were six stalls on either side of the aisle, and a beautiful equine head soon appeared over each wooden door, curiously surveying their visitors. Mandy beamed. She couldn't wait to be introduced to each and every one, but she saved a special smile for Cougar, whose box was the last on the right-hand side. Across the aisle was the only empty stall, but beside him he had China for company.

Mandy spotted a smaller door at the far end of the aisle. "Where does that lead to?"

"An open-fronted barn where we keep the hay and straw," said Paul, rummaging in the tack room. He came out and handed her some hard, molded shin pads with a soft lining and hefty Velcro fasteners. "These are the brushing boots. We'll use Fandango here as a model so you can see how to put them on."

Fandango's stall was first on the left. He was a wonderful bright chestnut color with a broad white blaze down his nose.

"Is Fandango a mustang, too?" Mandy wondered. "He looks a little like Cougar."

"He's part mustang," Paul answered. "He's eight — a couple of years older than Coug. But he doesn't act it!"

He crouched down to fit the first of the brushing boots. "We start by smoothing down the hair on the leg to make sure it's lying flat, then we fit the boot in place and fasten the straps," he explained. He closed the three Velcro straps and straightened up again. "You want the fasteners to be tight enough to stop the boot from slipping down over the horse's fetlock, but not so tight that it's uncomfortable when the horse moves around. Want to try the next one yourself?"

"I'm happy if Fandango's happy!" said Mandy. The horse shifted as Mandy bent down and she paused, not wanting to alarm him. She glanced up to find him watching her closely. Just as Paul had done, she smoothed down the hair on Fandango's slender leg and carefully fixed the protective boot into position.

"Excellent," said Paul. "Now I'll finish off Fandango. Why not introduce yourself to Izzy over there?" He gestured to a magnificent palomino two stalls down across

the aisle. "She's part quarter horse, twelve years old. She's very gentle."

"I can tell," said Mandy, going over to pet the animal's smooth, cream-colored neck. Izzy was certainly beautiful. But Mandy couldn't stop herself from glancing down the aisle at Cougar, who was watching her intently. She hoped Paul would let her fit the brushing boots on him, too!

Paul was a lot faster than Mandy — he could put boots on two horses in the time it took her to do one. He also fitted each horse with a halter as he went. In the end, there were just China and Cougar left.

"Aren't they still wearing their boots from their gallop in the fields?" Mandy wondered.

"I took them off," said Paul. "I thought I'd be out fixing up the paddocks with Lisa this afternoon." He winked at Mandy. "Want to see to Cougar?"

"Yes, please," said Mandy. "He's amazing!"

"He sure is," Paul agreed. "Though I've got a soft spot for China, too." He held out a hand to the black-and-white mare, letting her rub her head against it. "She was my first competition horse. I bought her as an unbroken three-year-old when I was just nineteen."

Mandy frowned. "Unbroken?"

"Sorry, I mean that no one had ridden or trained her before. You can't really start the process till the horse is three or four — strong enough to carry a rider and be ready to learn. . . ." He smiled. "And China sure was a fast learner. We won a bunch of Western riding competitions. Barrel racing's her specialty, while Cougar looks like he's going to be a good all-rounder."

"Will you be holding competitions here?" Mandy asked.

"Maybe," said Paul, unbolting the door to Cougar's stall and standing back to let Mandy go inside. "We've got all sorts of plans for Hart's Leap Ranch. Trail rides, equestrian classes, rodeo theme days . . ."

"I want to do *all* of those!" Mandy declared.

"Well, let's hope there's a lot of folks around here who feel the same," Paul said as he let himself into China's stall.

Cougar stood perfectly still as Mandy put on his brushing boots. To her delight, the mustang leaned down and softly sniffed her hair while she was fitting a boot on his foreleg. She felt as if they'd made friends already!

She heard Paul go out of the small door at the end of the aisle and come back a few moments later. "They're making a lot of progress with the fence," he reported. "We should be able to turn the horses out in another twenty minutes."

While they were waiting, and with the sound of hammering drifting into the yard, Paul showed Mandy around the rest of the buildings. Mandy was very impressed by all the work they had done so far. The old cowsheds had been converted into feed rooms and equipment stores; the first shed was lined with gleaming steel bins for the different types of feed, and the second shed had two walls filled with racks for waterproof rugs, stable blankets, and grooming kits.

"Will the horses need rugs if they're going outside?" Mandy asked.

Paul shook his head. "Not today. It's kind of mild now, and they'll only be out for a couple of hours. Besides, it's their first time out, so they'll probably run around more than usual to get rid of all that energy!"

"And if they're wearing rugs, they'll get too hot," Mandy said, realizing.

"That's right," said Paul. "While we wait for Lisa and James to finish up, would you like to help me fill the hay nets and water buckets for the horses' afternoon feed?"

"Yep!" said Mandy.

Paul led the way to the open-fronted barn. "Don't forget to shake the wedges of hay before you put them into the nets," he warned. "Make sure there are no twigs or stones caught in them."

He left Mandy stuffing the spacious bag-shaped nets and went to fill the water buckets. Mandy was just tightening the cord around the top of the last hay net when

James and Lisa appeared around the side of the horse barn.

"All done!" Lisa announced, looking pleased. "We made short work of fixing those rails. James has a real knack with a hammer and nails."

"I help out my dad with some home-improvement, sometimes," James said bashfully.

"Sounds like we're good to go!" Paul declared.

"Do all the horses get along OK?" asked Mandy. "Or do some of them need to be kept apart?"

"They're used to living together, back in San Antonio," Lisa explained. "We had three paddocks at the ranch there, so we've used the same setup to make them feel at home over here. We have a fourth paddock, too, that we could use if we buy any more horses."

Two of the paddocks were close to the yard, while the other two lay a little farther up the hill along a stony track. "We'll put four in the farthest field to start with," said Paul. "China, Izzy, Woody, and Wishful Thinking."

Paul and Lisa went into the barn and led out the horses. Mandy could tell from Woody's slender frame and delicate head that he was part-mustang like Fandango, with a chestnut coat. He was a little shorter than both Cougar and Fandango, and his black tail flicked lazily from side to side as he stepped forward. Wishful Thinking was a striking Morgan mare, jet-black with a white star between her eyes. Her mane was thick and silky, and she had the smallest, pointiest ears Mandy had ever seen.

"Want to give me a hand here, Mandy?" asked Lisa. "China and Izzy won't give you any trouble."

"Sure," she said eagerly, taking the horses' lead ropes.

Paul turned to James. "Well, partner, do you think you could help me turn out Chase, Loco, and Jackrabbit?"

"I'd love to," James said. He followed Paul inside and came out leading a chestnut gelding that was like Fandango, but with four white socks. He looked a little stockier, too, and Paul explained that he was part quarter horse, rather than mustang. "Chase is thirteen years old, so he's one of the older horses. He's a great horse for less experienced riders."

James grinned. "Sounds like my kind of horse!"

Mandy looked at the other two horses Paul had led out into the yard. He introduced them as Loco and Jackrabbit. Stocky Loco was straining forward on the lead rope, his short wiry coat spattered all over with brown-and-white patches. The bay gelding, Jackrabbit, swung his head from side to side as he took in his surroundings more calmly.

"Jackrabbit's the baby of the group," Lisa told Mandy as they all set off with their horses. "He's only five years old, but he's got a very wise head on those shoulders.

We've got high hopes for him as a competition horse."
Woody stopped dead, and Lisa tugged on his lead rope.
"There's no need to be jealous, Woody, we've got high
hopes for you, too!"

They led the horses along a broad grassy track to the
farthest gate, and took them into the paddock before
unbuckling their halters. Wishful Thinking cantered off
at once with her tail kinked over her back, but Izzy
dropped her head to pull at the thick green grass. Woody
and China wandered off to explore the fence on the
other side of the field.

"Well, they look happy enough," Lisa said decidedly.
She and Mandy walked back down the track to watch
James and Paul turn out their horses. As soon as Paul
took off Loco's halter, the spotted pony sprang away
and circled the field at top speed, tossing up chunks of
grass under his hooves.

Mandy grinned. "I bet he needs a firm rider."

"Loco's a funny one," said Lisa. "He bucks more than
any of our horses, but once it's out of his system, he's as
good as gold."

"Come on, let's go get the others," Paul urged. "They'll
be getting jealous if they can hear these guys having a
good time out here!"

"I bet I can guess who Mandy wants to lead out!" said

Lisa. "I don't blame you — Cougar's a very special horse. I'll turn out Bobcat, and James can take Fig."

"And I'll take Fandango." Paul led the way back to the horse barn. "We could sure use you two working around here full-time. It makes everything a whole lot quicker!"

"I guess you'll need a full-time staff when you open," Mandy said.

"In a couple of weeks," Paul agreed. "It was kind of difficult, finding people long-distance. We were hoping to have a grand opening in time for Easter, but there were delays with the builders."

"Still, now that we're here, things are running a lot more smoothly," said Lisa, entering the stables.

Fig and Bobcat were both quarter horse mares. Fig had a light brown coat with a black mane and tail; Bobcat was a little darker. Mandy could tell that Lisa had a soft spot for Bobcat from the way she ran her hand gently down her mane and whispered something Mandy couldn't hear. From the way Bobcat hooked her head over Lisa's shoulder, it was clear that the horse felt the same way.

While James led out Fig, Mandy took hold of Cougar's lead rope. He leaned against her and rubbed his lips gently across her shoulder.

"You *are* privileged," Lisa observed. "Cougar won't do that to just anyone."

Mandy felt very proud as she led the mustang outside. "Come on, boy," she told him. "Time to see your new home."

They led the three horses to the paddock halfway along the track, on the opposite side from the other horses. Mandy waited until Paul had closed the gate behind them before unbuckling Cougar's halter, just in case he made a dash for freedom. But he stood still for a few moments after she had taken it off, gazing around him with his beautiful ears pricked. Then he tossed his head, flicking his mane in a silky black wave, before spinning around and cantering across the grass, kicking up his back heels every few strides.

"Is he all right?" asked James, who had retreated to the other side of the gate.

Paul laughed. "He's having a great time! When a horse behaves like that, we say the grass is 'tickling their toes.'"

Mandy felt as if she could watch Cougar play forever. The other horses took no notice of him and put down their heads to graze.

She winced as a cold gust blew against the back of her head. It still stung just a bit, and she was starting to feel very tired. Lisa noticed. "How about you two go clean up and relax inside for a while, before we take you home?"

"I don't want to stop watching the horses," Mandy admitted.

Lisa smiled. "Don't worry, this won't be your only chance. In fact, I was thinking you two might like to come over for a ride on Tuesday. To say thanks for your help today."

"It was the least we could do when you rescued us in the mist," James pointed out.

"Honestly, we'd love for you to come," said Paul. "And if you go back to school and tell all your friends how cool Western-style riding is, it'll be good publicity for us!"

Mandy looked at James. "The thought of doing some real Western riding sounds fantastic."

Lisa grinned. "Especially if you're on Cougar, right?"

"Could I?" asked Mandy, her eyes wide.

"He's clearly comfortable around you. I think you'd both have a great time!"

"Can I ride Fig?" said James.

"Sure," said Paul. "Fig's great with beginners, too. As long as she doesn't think her rider's getting too big for his boots!"

"I promise that won't be the case with me," said James. "But I don't even *own* any riding boots!"

"We've got plenty of spare boots." Paul laughed. "What about you, Mandy?"

"Will it be OK to wear my regular riding clothes?" she asked.

Lisa nodded. "They'll be fine. Though actually, Western saddles are so comfy you can wear jeans instead of jodhpurs if you prefer."

Mandy paused for a moment to watch Cougar before following the others back down the track. His wheat-colored coat looked exotic and bright against the gray-and-green field rising up behind him, half hidden in mist. It was a strange but beautiful sight — like a little piece of cowboy life brought to Yorkshire.

"See you again soon," Mandy whispered to the mustang. "And that's a promise!"

Four

The next day, after a good night's sleep, Mandy's head felt much better. She was surprised to see that she had slept until eight-thirty. Last night she had been so excited at the thought of going back to Hart's Leap Ranch to see Cougar, she didn't think she would be able to sleep at all.

After checking on Sherpa, who was looking much more comfortable now that the antibiotics were starting to heal his infection, she headed for the kitchen.

"Have you seen my old jeans, Mom?" she asked, helping herself to some cereal. "I'll need them on Tuesday for riding Cougar."

Dr. Emily smiled. "Mustangs in Yorkshire — who would have thought it! You know, a Western horse deserves a special Western riding outfit. I think I have some leather chaps up in the attic somewhere. I wore them to a fancy costume party your dad and I went to at veterinary college, *years* ago." When Mandy frowned, she explained, "Chaps are like footless leggings you strap on over jeans, to make sitting in the saddle more comfortable. They look pretty stylish, too!"

"Can we find them?"

"What, right now?"

"Please?" Mandy begged.

Soon they were rummaging through boxes of old clothes in the dim light of the attic's single bulb.

"Here they are!" Dr. Emily cried in triumph, pulling out the promised chaps. "Gosh, I could never fit into these now. They could be just right for you, though, sweetie."

Mandy inspected them. They were brown leather and fringed with tasseled suede. "They're perfect!" she declared. "Thanks!" A thought occurred to her then. "Mom, if you went to the party as a cowboy, what was Dad dressed up as?"

Carefully keeping a straight face, Mandy's mom pulled out another outfit from the trunk. At first, Mandy thought it was an old rug. The fake orange fur was shapeless, very itchy looking, and dotted with brown spots. When Dr. Emily shook it out, Mandy realized there was a pair of tattered leopard-skin shorts stitched at the bottom.

She burst out laughing. "A caveman?"

Her mom nodded. "The theme of the party was things beginning with *C*," she recalled with a grin. "There were a lot of clowns and cowboys around, but your dad was the only caveman!"

"I'm not surprised," said Mandy.

Dr. Adam's head appeared through the hatch into the attic. "What's going on up here?"

"Reliving past glories," Dr. Emily replied, dangling the hairy caveman outfit at him.

"Good grief!" he cried. "You kept that?" Dr. Adam laughed. "Speaking of things beginning with *C*, I've left some antiseptic udder lotion for the herdsman over at Upper Welford Hall."

"That doesn't begin with *C*," teased Dr. Emily.

"For his sick *cow*," said Dr. Adam patiently.

"What was wrong with her?" Mandy asked.

"Mastitis. It's a fairly common infection, and she'll be fine after the treatment." He raised his eyebrows. "It's the rest of the animals I worry about, with Georgia and Max on the loose."

"Who are they?" said Mandy.

"Sam Western's great-niece and nephew. They're eight-year-old twins, staying with him for the spring break while their mother does some business in York — and they are quite a handful!"

Mandy bit her lip. "They're not mean to the animals, are they?"

"Oh, no, they love them to pieces," Dr. Adam assured her. "And they're dying to help take care of them — they just don't know how. Yesterday, they let out all the cows while they were waiting to be milked because they thought the exercise would do the animals good."

"I bet the herdsman was happy!" said Mandy, making a face.

"I suppose they mean well." Dr. Emily smiled.

"They do," said Dr. Adam. "Sam's promised to get them a special treat to keep them busy for the next two weeks — hopefully, it'll keep them out of trouble, too!"

To go with her chaps, Mandy decided to spend some of her allowance on a blue denim shirt. She had decided to get into the spirit of Western-style riding — and she'd be able to wear it with jeans for line dancing.

"I'm going into Walton on Monday morning to pick up some supplies for the residential unit," said Dr. Emily. "I'll drop you off and you can do some shopping."

"Thanks, Mom. For that, you're getting an extra big Easter present." Then Mandy frowned. "Oops. I haven't bought *anyone* an Easter present yet!"

"There's still plenty of time." Her mother smiled. "You can also do some holiday shopping while you're in Walton."

James joined them for the expedition. "I can't believe you're wearing those chaps to Walton!" he complained from the back of the Land Rover. Just then, the Cowboys' "Saddles and Spurs" played on the radio. "This should be your theme song!"

Mandy twisted around in the front seat to look at him. "What's wrong with my chaps?" she demanded. She had put them on over her jeans. They were still a little baggy, but not enough to cause discomfort. "I want to make sure my new shirt matches with them, that's all."

"You look like you're going to a line-dancing class," grumbled James. "I guess I should be glad you're not wearing your grandpa's Stetson as well!"

Dr. Emily dropped Mandy and James at the shopping mall while she went to get her vet supplies. Mandy stopped at Merry's candy store first. Her new legwear got a lot of attention from passersby. An elderly couple gave her curious stares, while a group of younger girls pointed and whispered to one another. A teenage boy grinned at her and called out, "Ride 'em, cowgirl!"

Mandy grinned. "Wait till they've heard about Hart's Leap Ranch," she said to James. "I bet half the town will be wearing chaps just like these before long!"

They found a young boy and girl browsing the display of chocolate Easter eggs in the candy store. "Every store's the same," the little girl complained. "Chicks and bunnies, that's all you can find."

"There should be more lambs," the boy piped up. He was blond-haired and blue-eyed, just like the girl, though his nose was a little more tilted up. "I bet Great-uncle Sam would love a chocolate lamb for Easter. As a thank-you for our present! Let's buy him one before he comes to get us."

Mandy turned to James, who was studying a selection of Easter egg chocolates. "I think I know who these two are. Back in a sec." She went over to introduce herself. "Excuse me," she said. "Your names wouldn't be Georgia and Max, would they?"

The boy stared at her. "How did you know?" Then he noticed her chaps and gasped. "Are you a real cowboy?"

"Don't be silly, Max," said Georgia. "There aren't any cowboys in Yorkshire!"

Mandy glanced at James, who smiled at her as if to say, *That's what* she *thinks*.

"My name's Mandy," she explained. "I know your great-uncle Sam. My dad is the vet who takes care of his animals — I think you met him yesterday. His name is Dr. Adam Hope."

"Your dad has a cool job," said Georgia. "I want to be a vet when I grow up. I'm really good at tending animals."

"So am I!" added Max.

"That's why Great-uncle Sam gave us such an awesome present," Georgia went on. "Twin lambs!"

"We named them Sooty and Sweep. Though they're not really ours to keep," said Max. "We're only here for two weeks."

"But one of Great-uncle Sam's friends had some three-week-old orphans!" Georgia broke in. "Since they don't have a mom anymore, we have to bottle-feed them."

Mandy frowned, partly at the flood of information that had just poured out, and partly because the twins seemed rather young to be hand-rearing lambs. "What are you feeding them?" she asked.

"Warm milk, four times a day," answered Georgia.

That sounded about right to Mandy, and she smiled. "I bet they're really sweet."

"They are," said Max. "And they're getting bigger every day. You should come and see them."

"Come see them tomorrow!" Georgia suggested.

"I'd like that." Mandy smiled. "But I'm busy tomorrow.

If it's OK with your great-uncle, maybe I could come later in the week."

"Will you come on your horse?" asked Max, wide-eyed.

"She's *not* a cowboy!" Georgia insisted. "Are you, Mandy?"

"I'm afraid not," she admitted.

"Did someone want chocolate lambs?" called James, waving a box. "They have some here!"

"Yeah!" cried Max. He beat Georgia in the rush to grab the box from James.

"You can come and see our lambs, too," Georgia told James, snatching the box from Max. "Quick, Max. Uncle Sam will be here in a minute!"

As the twins rushed off to buy their Easter gift, James turned to Mandy with a puzzled look. "Lambs?"

"It's a long story," said Mandy. "Let's buy our gifts first — then I'll tell you all about it!"

The shopping trip was successful, and Mandy returned to Animal Ark with several bags full of chocolate eggs and bunnies and a brand-new denim shirt with white embroidered stitching. After she had unpacked her shopping, Mandy found herself wishing the hours away. She knew she should be making the most of her vacation, but she couldn't wait to be back with Cougar and all the other horses.

She spent lots of time with Sherpa in the residential area. He was getting better every day, eating well and even batting a pom-pom on a string Mandy had made for him to play with.

By the time Tuesday morning came around, Mandy was fizzing with excitement. She woke early and dressed in her Western riding gear before breakfast. Her new deep-blue denim shirt looked really good next to the dark brown chaps with her faded jeans underneath.

Dr. Adam was happy to give Mandy a lift to Hart's Leap Ranch. "I must confess," he said, "I'm very curious to see their setup!"

They picked up James on the way. Mandy was surprised to see him wearing a black cowboy hat, a plaid shirt, and a slightly baggy suede vest!

"I didn't think you should have all the fun!" He grinned. "My mom picked up the hat at a costume store, and the vest is a hand-me-down from a cousin. I never thought I'd actually wear it!"

"What about the shirt?" said Mandy. "Is that from a costume shop, too?"

"This is *my* shirt!" he protested. "Watch out, or I won't tell you what I found out about mustangs on the Internet."

"What did it say?" Mandy asked, interested at once.

"Apparently, mustangs were brought to North

America by the Spanish in the sixteenth century," he explained. "They were the best horses the Spanish had, bred from Arabian ponies, Andalusians, and North African Barbs. The Native Americans had never seen anything like them — over there, horses had become extinct about ten thousand years earlier."

' Mandy raised her eyebrows. "Imagine never having seen a horse!"

"The Spanish didn't allow the Native Americans to own or ride horses at first. But when they caught some that had escaped into the wild, it changed their way of life forever. They became hunters and warriors and lived far better lives — all thanks to mustangs like Cougar!"

"Cougar would make *anyone's* life better," Mandy agreed.

The Land Rover rumbled along the narrow road that led into the next valley. At last, Dr. Adam slowed the car and turned on his left turn signal. "This is new," he remarked as they turned onto a white graveled drive. "This used to be a dirt road, churned up by tractors."

"There's going to be a big entrance sign up soon," James told him. "Paul and Lisa have renamed the farm Hart's Leap Ranch."

"Well, there aren't many ranches in Yorkshire, so that should stand out well," said Dr. Adam.

He followed Mandy and James to the front door to

introduce himself to the Cookes, and thank them for looking after Mandy and James on Saturday.

"They were great to have around," said Paul, grasping Dr. Adam's hand in a firm handshake. "Looking forward to a ride, guys?"

"Are we ever!" said Mandy.

"You sure look the part," said Lisa. "Nice shirt, Mandy — and the cowboy hat really suits you, James!"

"I'm glad we've met you, Adam," said Paul. "We're sure all our horses are fine, but we'd love for you to run a professional eye over them before we open. I'd ask you right now, but we're expecting some other visitors shortly."

Mandy wondered who else was coming since the ranch wasn't officially open yet.

"I'm in a little rush myself this morning," said Dr. Adam. "But call the clinic and make an appointment. I'm sure my wife would love to come, too! Some time next week maybe?"

"Sounds great," said Paul. "We'll see you!"

Mandy and James followed the Cookes inside. James excused himself to go to the bathroom.

"Do you want a snack or a drink before we saddle up, Mandy?" asked Lisa.

"Just a glass of water," she said, a little distracted. What if the other visitors wanted to ride Cougar as well?

James came back into the kitchen. "I love the poster you've got in the hall for *Plains Rider*," he said. "I saw that movie twice!"

"Did you recognize anyone?" asked Paul with a twinkle in his eye. "Aside from the actors, I mean."

James ducked back out to take a look, and Mandy went to join him. The framed poster was advertising last year's big Western. Behind the close-ups of the stars, a group of cowboys galloped through a cactus-strewn landscape, kicking up dramatic clouds of dust.

Mandy's eyes widened as she studied one of the horses. The gorgeous chestnut coat and the broad white blaze down the horse's nose were unmistakable. "That looks just like Fandango!"

James pointed to a handsome buckskin horse rearing up in the background. "And that could be Bobcat!"

Mandy realized he was right. The rider's face was half-hidden by a bandanna but Mandy was sure she recognized the eyes. "Is that *you* riding her, Lisa?" she demanded, turning to face her as Lisa stood in the doorway to the kitchen.

"Sure is," Lisa admitted. "I couldn't believe I made it onto the poster. I was only an extra."

"Whoa!" cried James. "You're famous!"

She laughed. "The horses are the stars, believe me! Paul and I used to be stunt riders. We started out in

rodeos and moved on to movies. That's actually how we met."

Paul nodded. "I had to fall from my horse in front of her sixteen times in a row while shooting *Midnight West Rustlers*. Guess I fell for Lisa at the same time!"

"But I thought you ran a riding center in San Antonio," said Mandy.

"That's what we went on to do together," said Lisa. "We got tired of spending so much time apart filming in different places. But we both loved horses, so we set up the ranch. We still do a little movie work, but only as a sideline."

"It was the money from *Plains Rider* that paid for most of our move over here," Paul added.

"I doubt you'll be doing much film work here, will you?" said James. "I mean, they don't shoot many Westerns in Yorkshire!"

"You'd be surprised," Paul said mysteriously. "The visitors we're expecting today are from a music video company. They're checking out the ranch and the horses for a shoot later this week for the new Cowboys' single."

Mandy stared at him. "The Cowboys are filming a video *here*?"

"Booked for Friday," Paul confirmed.

"So *that's* why you canceled the regular line-dance class!" James figured.

"That's so cool!" Mandy said.

Lisa smiled. "Are you a Cowboys fan?"

Mandy nodded. "I love their last song, 'Saddles and Spurs.'"

"The new single's even better," said Paul. "It's called 'Riding a Storm.' They want an authentic Western feel to the video, and we've got all the tack and horses they need!"

A worrying thought nagged at Mandy. "If the video people are coming today, can we still ride?"

"Of course," said Lisa. "In fact, I'm sure they'd love to see a couple of the horses in action!"

There was the sound of tires on the gravel outside, and Paul went into the kitchen to look out of the window. "Looks like they're here right now!" he called. "And it's not just the director and the girl from the record company."

"Who else, then?" called Lisa.

Paul was smiling broadly as he came back to join them. "Only Mitch McFadden!"

James frowned. "Who?"

"Mitch McFadden?" Mandy gasped. "He's the Cowboys' lead singer! He's like, the most famous pop star in the world right now! I can't believe we're actually going to meet him!"

Five

When Paul opened the front door, a young woman in a black pantsuit with short red hair and frameless glasses stood there, smiling. "Hi. I'm Vicki Baker, Band Liaison," she said.

"Paul Cooke. And this is my wife, Lisa. Come on in," said Paul.

Vicki Baker stepped inside and gestured behind her to a bald man with dark glasses and an earring. "This is Jason Caine. He'll be directing the video."

"Let's see the horses," said Jason Caine, stony-faced as he pushed into the hall.

"He has another appointment to get to," Vicki

explained with an apologetic smile. "And this is my client —"

"Hi, I'm Mitch." A young man with wavy blond hair and blue eyes offered his hand to Paul and Lisa.

Mandy knew she was staring with her mouth open, but Mitch McFadden was even more handsome in real life than he was in the posters.

"He's not as tall as I thought he would be," James whispered, and Mandy shushed him.

"Great-looking place you have here," said Mitch. "I grew up on a farm myself."

"Do you ride?" asked Lisa.

"Not for years," he confessed. "I used to be a junior show jumper. I had to give it up before I made any senior teams, but I had a lot of fun — and met a lot of special horses."

"Sorry," said Jason Caine, "but could we hurry it up?" He paused when he saw Mandy and James. "Are these your kids?"

"Uh, no. They're a couple of ranch hands," said Paul. "Mandy and James."

"Hi," Mandy said shyly, and James mumbled a hello.

Vicki gave them a little wave, and Mitch smiled across at them. "Dressed like that, I thought they were here to audition!"

"So, the horses?" Jason Caine asked curtly.

"They're all in the barn, ready and waiting," said Lisa. She led Mr. Caine out the back door.

"I know Mitch would like to see the horses, too," said Vicki. "Perhaps in the meantime, Paul, you and I could go over the contracts?"

Mitch smiled at Mandy and James. "Since Jason's steamed on ahead, how about you guys show me around?"

"Sure!" Mandy turned to Paul. "If that's OK with you?"

Paul grinned. "Be my guest."

"I can't believe this is happening," Mandy whispered as she and James led the way out to the yard.

"Just be cool," James advised her. But then he tripped over a loose stone and almost fell flat on his face.

"Right," Mandy said. "I'll be cool!"

"Are you really ranch hands?" said Mitch. "If you don't mind me saying so, you look a little young to be working full-time!"

Mandy laughed; it was easy to forget that Mitch was an international superstar when he seemed like such a regular person. "We helped Paul and Lisa with some fencing the other day," she told him, "and they offered us a free ride in return."

"So, you ride Western style, right?" said Mitch.

"Only once, and that was just down the trail," Mandy admitted. "Today will be my first real try."

"Well, it's quite an experience." Mitch smiled. "I wish I had more time for riding, but life's pretty busy in the band. We're only in Yorkshire for a few days, doing some local TV spots."

"Your friend Jason doesn't seem to have much time, either," observed James.

"He's not my friend, he just directed our last video," said Mitch. "It's been shown a lot, so the record company is using him again. I just hope he's better dealing with horses than he is with people!"

"I'm sure he will be," Mandy said. She changed back to her favorite subject. "Did you have your own horse when you were a show jumper?"

"Yep. Her name was Tigra. She was stunning — part Arab and part Thoroughbred, very pale beige with a black mane and tail. She was a natural and could jump higher than her ears when she was in the right mood." He sighed. "Unfortunately, she hit a fence at a qualifying jumping match and chipped a bone in her leg. She pulled through, but it ended her career in the ring."

"I'm sorry," Mandy murmured, feeling a rush of sympathy because Mitch looked so sad.

He shrugged as if he were trying to pull himself back to the present. "Well, it was a long time ago."

When they entered the barn, they found Jason Caine

inspecting the horses with Lisa. "We'll have the ginger one for sure," he said to Lisa.

"You mean Fandango?"

"I guess. The ginger one."

Lisa looked hesitant. "He's not an easy ride, so unless the band members are experienced riders —"

"Look, I want the ginger one, OK?" snapped Mr. Caine. "The only one from the band who'll be riding is Mitch. The others will hang around in the background while your stunt riders do their stuff." He paused. "You *are* still able to provide the stunt riders?"

"No problem," said Lisa, sounding a little tense.

"I want that tan-colored one, too," Jason went on, taking another couple of pictures. "Sleek but kind of tough looking. I like that."

"Cougar?" Lisa checked. "Sure."

"He's beautiful," Mitch breathed, walking up to the stall for a closer look. "And that buckskin coat is just like Tigra's!"

"He's a pure mustang," Mandy announced, feeling thrilled that Mitch had picked out her favorite.

"I'd like to check out the locations around here now, and see if we can get some interesting camera angles," said Jason Caine.

"There's an excellent view of Axwith Tor from halfway up the hill," said Lisa. "I'll show you." She raised her eyebrows at Mandy and James. "Do you guys mind waiting here for a few minutes? I'll start tacking up when I've finished with Mr. Caine."

"Could I brush Cougar while we're waiting?" Mandy asked.

"Sure," said Lisa.

"Why don't you let me saddle Cougar for you?" Mitch offered. "I've ridden in the States enough times to know my way around Western tack, and it might mean these guys get out on their ride sooner."

Lisa smiled. "Well, if you don't mind, that would be great. Thanks. You'll find everything you need in the tack room."

"Let's get a move on," demanded Jason Caine, and he marched off down the aisle. With a shrug, Lisa followed him.

Still not quite believing that a rock star was tacking up a pony for her, Mandy buckled Cougar's halter onto his delicate head and tied him to the ring on the wall of his stable. She brushed his coat until it was clean and smooth, and was just untangling the knots in his tail when Mitch returned with a large, cherry-red saddle. James followed with the bridle slung over his shoulder and a folded saddle blanket in his arms. Mandy smiled

to herself as she thought how Sam Western's great-nephew Max would refuse to believe James wasn't a cowboy if he could see him right now!

"Can you do the honors with the blanket, James?" said Mitch.

James unfolded the blanket and laid it well forward on the mustang's back, then pulled it back until the front was resting at Cougar's withers. Meanwhile, Mitch rested the saddle on the stable door and started to arrange the leather straps that were hanging down. When he noticed Mandy watching him curiously, he explained what he was doing. "You have to lay the cinches — that's these thick straps here — and the breast collar over the seat, then hook the right stirrup over the saddle horn."

"I get it," Mandy said. "That stops them from hitting Cougar's sides and makes sure they can't get caught underneath the saddle as you put it on his back."

"Right. Then you pick up the saddle so the fork is in your left hand, and approach the horse from front left so he can see you coming."

"What's the fork?" asked James, who had finished straightening the blanket.

"The front of the saddle," said Mitch. He lifted the heavy saddle onto Cougar's back, then, keeping one hand on the horse's tail end, so that Cougar always knew where he was, he walked behind the mustang to check all around the saddle area. "There should be an inch or so of blanket showing all the way around," he said. "And be careful where you place the saddle. Too far forward and you'll interfere with the horse's movement. Too far the other way and you could bruise his back."

Mandy ran her hand down Cougar's neck, underneath his mane. "I'd never hurt you," she whispered.

"Now we let down the cinches and the stirrups," said Mitch.

Mandy pulled the thick leather straps down so they hung over Cougar's sides. He blew through his nose at her, and she smiled.

"Let's tighten the front cinch first," Mitch instructed. "Remember, most horses will suck in air to stop you from tightening the saddle too much to begin with, so take it nice and slow."

Mandy watched as he skillfully looped the leather straps through the different buckles and rings. She couldn't believe she was having a lesson in saddling up from a famous pop star! He seemed so down-to-earth and ordinary, and his love for horses was evident.

"Mitch?" Vicki Baker appeared at the end of the aisle, holding out a tiny cell phone. "I've got Dales Stadium on the phone, wanting to talk through the songs for your acoustic set tomorrow."

Mitch sighed and patted Cougar. "Guess I live in another world now," he said, a touch of regret in his voice. "That was fun, guys. Sorry I couldn't finish the lesson. Maybe if you're around on the day of the shoot, we'll pick up where we left off."

"You'd let us watch the shoot?" Mandy asked.

"Why wouldn't I?" He waved good-bye. "Just don't wear that mustang out before Friday, you hear? I can't wait to ride Cougar myself."

Mandy knew she was grinning from ear to ear. "Mitch McFadden just asked us to come to his video shoot! I must be dreaming!"

"Want me to pinch you?" James offered.

Cougar tossed his head impatiently, as if wondering where all his attention had gone. Mandy laughed. "Cougar, you're going to be a star!"

As soon as Jason Caine had soon seen everything he wanted to, he whisked Mitch and Vicki away in his luxury sedan. Paul and Lisa came back to the barn looking rather solemn.

"What a difficult man." Lisa sighed as she finished tightening Cougar's girth.

Paul was saddling up Fig, getting him ready for

James's riding lesson. "He's not so bad," he called from the stable farther down the aisle. "And the shoot gives us a great chance to see Frank and Jodie again."

"Who are they?" asked James.

"Friends from our stunt-riding days," Paul explained. "It's perfect timing — they're taking a European vacation, and offered to help us out in exchange for room and board for a few days! They'll gallop around Saturday's shoot, making Mitch and the guys look amazing."

"And I hear you've been invited to watch," said Lisa. Lifting the headpiece of the bridle over Cougar's ears with her right hand, she slotted the bit into his mouth with her left.

"You don't mind us coming back again, do you?" Mandy checked. "We don't want to get in the way."

Paul chuckled. "Seeing how good you both are at saddling up, I bet we could use your help setting up that morning!"

"We'll be here anytime you want us," said Mandy. "Won't we, James?"

He nodded eagerly. "Just imagine what they'll say at school when we tell them we watched the new Cowboys video being made!"

"And it'll be more good publicity for Hart's Leap Ranch," Mandy added.

"You're right there," said Lisa. "Well, these horses are

ready. We'll go saddle up China and Bobcat, and then get riding!"

Soon they had all mounted up and were setting off across the countryside in the sunshine. At first, they rode slowly but soon speeded up to a canter. Today, the big Western saddle didn't feel so strange to Mandy, and she sat back with her feet resting lightly in the stirrups, enjoying Cougar's comfortable paces. There was no mist today and the view was amazing, a patchwork of fields stretching in all directions in a hundred different shades of green.

Cougar tossed his head, snorting with excitement. He wanted to look at everything — a plastic bag caught in a hedge, a flowering bush, a flock of noisy sheep. It made Mandy realize just how strange the new environment must seem to him! But despite all the distractions, she felt totally safe on his back.

"That's right, Mandy, nice and easy on the reins," said Lisa when they had slowed to a walk, giving Paul and Lisa a chance to watch their riding. "A lot of people assume that you turn the horse by pulling his head around with the reins. But in Western riding, it's the weight of the reins against the horse's neck combined with the pressure of your legs against his sides that turns him."

Paul was keeping an eye on James. "Try to keep your

eyes up as you ride," he suggested. "There's no need to watch Fig, she's taking care of you just fine — and you're missing the view!"

"Coug's really comfortable taking commands from you," Lisa said to Mandy. "See the position of his ears? They're relaxed, half-pricked. Loco and Fandango sometimes ride with their ears pinned back — which means they've heard what their rider's saying, but that they're not going to listen!"

James checked the position of Fig's ears. "She seems to be listening. Let's see." He kicked lightly behind the girth. "Canter up!" he cried, and Fig leaped forward obediently. James gave a loud whoop. "This is amazing!"

Mandy laughed as she joined the others chasing after him. She had been to other riding centers in the Walton area, but none of them could match the Western experience in sheer color and fun! "I think Hart's Leap Ranch is going to be very successful," Mandy told Cougar happily when they had slowed down again. "And I bet you'll be the most popular ride of them all."

"Especially once he's a world-famous star," said James. "*Meet Cougar, as ridden by Mitch McFadden of the* Cowboys!" he said in a mock-announcer tone.

"He's a star *whoever* is riding him!" Mandy insisted. The fields stretched temptingly beside the path so she pushed the mustang into a gallop, using the weight of the rein to steer him in a large circle. Paul and Lisa clapped and whistled, but Mandy could barely hear above the wind in her ears and the thundering of Cougar's hooves. If this was what being a cowboy was like, Mandy was almost tempted to give up her dream of becoming a vet!

Six

When Mandy woke up at home the next morning, Cougar was the first thing she thought of. After the ride yesterday she had washed him down before her dad had come to get her and James. Her shirt, draped over the back of her chair, was still covered in hairs that had been shed from his buckskin coat.

"I suppose I'll just have to pine for you until Saturday." She sighed.

"Mandy!" called her mom from downstairs. "Sherpa's owner is coming to get him soon if you want to say good-bye!"

"Coming!" said Mandy, rushing to get dressed.

Sherpa's striped tail coiled and uncoiled like a furry snake when Mandy burst into the residential unit, and he purred loudly while she opened his cage door.

"I say you're definitely ready to go home!" Mandy told him as she lifted him out.

The cat was picked up by Mrs. Chitty, a kind-faced older woman whose eyes lit up when she saw Sherpa looking so well.

"Try to keep his diet low on protein and phosphorus," Dr. Emily told the woman. "That way, his kidneys will have less to filter, and it will reduce the risk of the infection returning."

"Another satisfied customer," Mandy said happily when Mrs. Chitty had gone.

"Want to come with me to see if we've got another one?" Dr. Emily asked. "Your dad's in surgery all day, so he's asked me to check on the cow at Upper Welford Hall."

"Sure," Mandy said. "Can we take James, too? Then we can see Sooty and Sweep."

Emily Hope frowned, confused.

Mandy laughed. "Sooty and Sweep are the twins' lambs. I can't believe I didn't tell you!"

Mrs. Hope shook her head. "I can! All you've talked about lately are mustangs, line dances, and riding the range!"

*   *   *

Mandy had to laugh when she saw James limping toward their car with a pained expression.

"It was all that riding yesterday," he groaned. "I'm not used to it."

When they arrived at the Upper Welford Hall, Sam Western was just leaving in his silver-gray Land Rover. He opened the window and leaned out. "Dennis will help with you today," he told Dr. Emily. "I'm off to the York livestock sale."

"Are Georgia and Max around?" Mandy asked.

Mr. Western closed his eyes briefly as if he had a headache. "Yes, they're around all right. One of the farmhands is probably trying to stop them milking all my cows to feed their lambs!"

With that, he drove away. As Dr. Emily parked the Land Rover, Dennis Saville, Sam Western's farm manager, came out of a nearby barn and waved to them. Mandy and James were about to follow Dr. Emily over to meet him when they heard excited shouts behind them.

"It's Mandy and James!" cried Max, appearing from behind a cowshed.

Georgia was close behind him. "Hey, guys!" she called. "You're just in time to watch us feed Sooty and Sweep!"

"Great," said Mandy. "We were really looking forward to meeting them."

"How come you're not dressed as a cowboy today?" Max asked Mandy.

"For the millionth time, she's not a cowboy!" said Georgia. "I'm going to get the milk. See you over there!"

As Georgia ran off back to the cowshed, her blond hair streaming behind her, James turned to Max. "Where are the lambs?"

"In a pig sty, in the old part of the farmyard," Max explained. "Great-uncle Sam said he's been meaning to knock it down for years, but it's perfect for Sooty and Sweep! They sleep in the covered part and come out to play in the little pen. Come on, I'll show you!"

Mandy and James followed him into a paved yard, much smaller than the main yard. On the far side was a row of pig sties built from faded red brick. They looked very old-fashioned compared with the rest of the farm buildings, but they looked clean and comfortable, and there were no tiles missing from the slate roof. Just as Max had said, there was an open area in front of each sty enclosed by a low brick wall, so the pigs could get some fresh air whenever they wanted.

The sties looked pretty well suited to lambs, too! Mandy saw two fluffy shapes leaping about in front of the nearest sty. They started giving high-pitched little bleats as Max approached.

"They're adorable!" said Mandy.

"That one is Sooty," said Max, pointing to a gray-black bundle of wool that practically turned a cartwheel as Mandy and James leaned over the wall to pet him. "And that one's Sweep."

"He looks as smoky as a real chimney sweep!" joked James. Sweep was creamy-white with a gray face and a jet-black nose. His furry tail swung back and forth as he came up to say hello, nibbling gently at Mandy's fingers.

Mandy's heart melted. She loved all baby animals, but lambs were definitely her favorite. "Sorry, Sweep, I didn't bring any treats," she said. She straightened up and turned to Max. "They seem pretty hungry! They must love mealtimes."

Max nodded. "We give them warm milk four times a day. Georgia mixes up some special milk powder."

Georgia appeared at that moment, carrying two clear plastic bottles filled with milk. "It's time, little babies!" she cried, running toward the sty.

The two lambs hopped about the yard as if their toes were on fire.

Georgia opened the door to the sty, and she and her brother squeezed into the little yard.

"They're certainly lively, aren't they?" James commented, as the lambs bustled around the twins, latching

onto the bottles of milk with their tails whizzing in circles.

Mandy nodded distractedly. Now that the little animals were standing in one place, she could see that their tails and hind legs were quite soiled.

"It looks like they've been scouring," she remarked quietly.

James frowned. "Scouring?"

"It's when young animals get diarrhea," Mandy explained.

James wrinkled his nose. "You learn some lovely words growing up in a veterinary clinic, don't you?"

"Oh, no!" said Max, as Sweep gulped down the last of his milk. "Sweep's gotten himself messy again!"

"Has that been happening a lot?" Mandy asked.

"It's not their fault!" Georgia protested. "They're just babies. I'll get a sponge and clean them up."

"She washes them every afternoon," Max told James and Mandy.

"Mandy, James, I'm ready to go!" Dr. Emily called from the edge of the old yard.

Georgia pouted. "Do you have to leave already?"

"Mom's got another appointment," said Mandy. "But thanks for letting us watch you feed Sooty and Sweep."

"Come back soon!" said Max.

"The cow's doing well," said Dr. Emily once Mandy

and James were back in the Land Rover. "How were the lambs?"

"Very bouncy," said James.

"The twins seem devoted to them," Mandy added. "A fleece wash each afternoon and warm milk four times a day."

"Those lambs are old enough to start being weaned on to hard feed," said Dr. Emily. "They need grain and hay so that they're ready to eat grass when they go back to their flock. They'll also need plenty of fresh drinking water."

Mandy pictured the sty. "I didn't see a drinking trough."

"I'm sure Mr. Saville is keeping an eye on everything," said James.

"But it's a very busy time of year on the farm," Mandy fretted. "Georgia and Max could be taking care of Sooty and Sweep all by themselves."

Dr. Emily raised her eyebrows. "Hand-reared lambs can get too used to being looked after by people, and will get confused when they're put back in the flock. Sooty and Sweep have to get used to other sheep again as soon as possible." She sighed. "You know, I'm not sure Sam Western really thought through this gift of his."

"Can't you have a look at the lambs, Mom?" Mandy asked.

"I can't just invite myself to the farm to start randomly

checking Mr. Western's livestock," Dr. Emily reminded
her gently. "I'm a vet, not an animal inspector. Do you
think the lambs seemed happy?"

"Yes, they looked healthy enough, apart from some
scouring. But it's a big responsibility, weaning two animals." Mandy turned to James. "Maybe we could look
on the Internet for some articles to help Max and
Georgia. Hints and tips on hand-rearing lambs, that sort
of thing."

"Good idea," he agreed.

"And I'll ask Jean to dig out some back issues of our
veterinary journals if she's not too busy," Dr. Emily
promised.

Jean Knox was Animal Ark's efficient receptionist, and
the thought made Mandy smile. "She'll probably find me
a whole stack of articles, piled right up to the ceiling!"

Mandy and James had a very interesting afternoon,
learning all sorts of things about lambs and looking at
some really sweet pictures. They went to see Dillon
Lewis, too, a boy in their class who had helped care for
a lamb called Snowy at Woodbridge Farm Park. But he
was out with his older brother.

After saying good-bye to James until tomorrow,
Mandy walked home for supper. Her legs were aching,

and she wished she had Cougar with her to ride back to Animal Ark!

She was still daydreaming about galloping down Main Street in full Western attire, when she reached the front door. The telephone started ringing as soon as she stepped into the hall, and she picked it up. "Hello?"

"Hello, Mandy, dear," came her grandmother's familiar voice. "How are you?"

"A little tired, actually," Mandy admitted.

"Oh, dear," said Gran. "Does that mean you don't want to go line dancing tonight?"

"Oh, no!" cried Mandy. "I'd love to!"

"Good!" Gran chuckled. "We'll pick you up at six-thirty. But I'm afraid you'll have to bring your own Stetson — your grandpa's seems stuck to his head these days!"

Mandy put down the phone with a smile, then called James.

"Hi," he said. "Did you forget something?"

"Only that there's a line-dancing class in Walton tonight," Mandy told him. "Want to come?"

"Sorry, Mandy, but my legs can't take any more," said James. "I'll exercise my mind instead, sorting through the information we found."

"Good thinking," Mandy said. "I'll see if my mom or dad can give us a lift to see Sooty and Sweep tomorrow."

She went over to the reception desk to find that Jean Knox was just leaving for the day.

"I left out some lambing articles for you," she said, peering at Mandy over her glasses. "They're on my desk."

"Thanks, Jean!" Mandy picked up a small pile of magazines marked with notes. "By the way, would you like to come to a line-dancing class tonight? It's a lot of fun."

"Me?" Jean blinked. Then she laughed. "Sorry, Mandy, I'm afraid I've got two left feet! I love that toe-tapping music, though."

"Me, too," said Mandy, hugging the magazines to her chest. "I'll get you a copy of Paul and Lisa's CD as a thank-you for finding these articles!" She was certainly in the mood for dancing, now that she and James had gathered together enough tips to make Sooty and Sweep the healthiest lambs in Yorkshire.

Mandy flipped through some of the articles while scarfing down a cheese sandwich.

"Is it smart to dance with a full stomach?" Dr. Adam wondered aloud.

"It's only a snack," Mandy told him. "I need energy for all that dancing! By the way, can you take James and me to Upper Welford Farm tomorrow?"

Dr. Adam made a face. "Sorry, Mandy, but I'm very

busy tomorrow. And your mom's out on calls until the late afternoon."

"And James's parents will be at work. . . ." Mandy thought for a moment. "Maybe we could ride our bicycles?"

"It's more than four miles and steep hills all the way," Dr. Adam pointed out. "How concerned are you about those lambs?"

"I just want to make sure they'll be weaned by the end of next week," Mandy said. "Also, keeping busy makes the time go faster."

"Of course, you're counting down the days until the video shoot!" Dr. Adam realized, just as a toot on a horn outside told them that Gran and Grandpa had arrived. "Well, keep going at this pace and it'll be Friday in the blink of an eye!"

"Hope so!" Mandy grinned as she grabbed one of the magazines, slipped on her jacket, and ran to the front door. "I can't wait to see Mitch McFadden riding Cougar. Bye!"

Grandpa Hope was wearing his Stetson in the car, even though the top was squashed against the roof. "I can turn my head from side to side, but the hat stays right where it is!" He chuckled, demonstrating and making Mandy laugh.

"What are you reading, dear?" Gran asked, noticing the magazine in her lap.

"Sam Western's great-niece and nephew are hand-rearing some lambs. James and I are bicycling over tomorrow with some tips."

Grandpa frowned. "That's a long trip by bike. I'm heading that way tomorrow morning to pick up some seedlings from the Axbridge Nurseries. I'll give you a ride if you want."

"You're the best, Grandpa!" Mandy beamed. "That means I don't have to spare my legs tonight — I can really dance up a storm!"

Mandy was even more relieved about Grandpa's ride when she realized there were far fewer beginners in this class, and the tempo was a lot faster. Luckily, they were dancing to her favorite Cowboys album, and she had no trouble picking up the beat. Lisa and Paul even called her to the front of the class to demonstrate some new moves.

"This little lady is light on her feet!" said Paul, turning down the music for a moment. "So she can show us some pigeon toes. Start with your feet together, Mandy, then swivel on the balls of your feet to separate your heels. There you go!"

"We're going to follow that with a heel stomp!" Lisa

told the class. "Bend at the knees and raise both heels off the floor, then put them back down. Easy so far, right, Mandy?"

Mandy smiled. "I *think* so!"

"Now we're going to put both those moves together, each to a single beat of the music!" called Paul. "Let's try one of each at the end of a scissor step, OK, Mandy? We'll all clap you a rhythm. Ready, class? Let's go!"

Taking a deep breath and placing her feet together, Mandy danced along, accompanied by the steady claps from the watching students. She jumped with her feet apart, jumped again with a right-over-left cross step, then jumped and brought both feet back together. Then she swung her heels apart — but forgot to bend her knees and jumped on tiptoes instead.

"Good try!" cried Paul. "Keep clapping, we'll try it one more time!"

This time Mandy performed the steps perfectly. The rhythmic claps became a round of applause as she returned, red-faced but smiling, to her place in the line beside Gran.

"Now we're going to do that to some music," said Lisa. "And what better accompaniment than the new single from the Cowboys, 'Riding a Storm'!"

Mandy cheered as the music started. She lost her place a few times, listening to the words instead of

focusing on her feet. But as the soaring, catchy melody **filled the** hall, Mandy knew that the sight of Cougar, Fandango, and the other horses in action would make for a very special video.

At the end of the class, Mandy dashed over to Paul and Lisa. "Is it still OK if I come over on Friday?"

"Absolutely — we're counting on you!" Paul told her. "In fact, we were wondering if you'd like to come over tomorrow afternoon to help us get the horses ready."

"James, too, if he's up for it," Lisa added. "I can come and get you."

"Are you sure?" Mandy gasped.

Paul smiled. "It's the least we can do for our volunteers!"

"That would be perfect," Mandy beamed.

"In that case, we'll see you at two-thirty tomorrow!"

Mandy left the hall in high spirits. With lambs in the morning and mustangs in the afternoon, tomorrow was shaping up to be the busiest day of the vacation so far!

Seven

The next morning, Mandy and James walked excitedly toward the old part of Sam Western's farmyard, armed with a stack of magazines and printouts.

"I hope the twins are around," said James.

"We can always leave the articles with Dennis or one of the farmhands," Mandy pointed out. "Grandpa will be back in an hour."

Just then, Dennis Saville came into the yard with a sack of feed over his shoulder. He saw Mandy and James, but when they waved, he simply nodded and headed into one of the cowsheds.

"It doesn't look like he's in a very good mood," Mandy remarked.

"That could mean the twins *are* around," James guessed mischievously.

Mandy had been looking forward to seeing the lambs ever since their last visit, but when they reached the sty, her heart sank. Just like before, Sooty and Sweep were leaping around in the yard, but this time their bleating seemed more high-pitched and urgent when they ran over to the wall, and their hindquarters looked even dirtier than the day before.

"They're still scouring," Mandy said. "And there's no water trough in their pen."

James frowned. "But if they've got upset stomachs, shouldn't they be getting skinnier? I'm sure they look fatter than they did yesterday."

"I think they might be bloated," Mandy said, letting herself into the pen. "Something's definitely not right."

Just then Max and Georgia appeared from behind the nearest cowshed. "Hey, it's Mandy and James!" cried Max.

"Hi, guys!" Georgia called. When she saw Sooty and Sweep jumping around Mandy, she shook her head like a weary mother. "Greedy babies! You've only just had a snack and already you want another one."

"Hi, Max. Hello, Georgia." Mandy bent down and ran her hands over the lambs' stomachs. They felt hard and full, which was a sure sign of trapped air. "There doesn't seem to be any fresh water in Sooty and Sweep's pen," she said carefully.

"They don't need water," said Max.

"They only need milk," Georgia added. "Like human babies!"

"But babies only drink milk until they're old enough to eat real food," said James. "And animals grow up much faster than humans! They need lots of water and a little regular food so they can be weaned *off* the milk."

Mandy nodded. "I think these lambs may have some problems with their digestion. See the way their tummies look bloated?"

"That just means they love all the milk we're giving them!" Georgia protested, reaching over to rub Sweep's head.

Max tried to see the magazines James was holding. "Did you bring some comics?"

"Uh, no," said James. "These are articles about weaning lambs by hand. We thought they might be helpful."

"But Georgia knows all about raising lambs," said Max. "You're as bad as Great-uncle Sam! He was asking all sorts of questions this morning."

"Guys, you have to remember that when you go back home, so will Sooty and Sweep," Mandy said gently. "They'll be part of a flock again and they have to get used to feeding themselves."

"I thought you were nice," Georgia sulked. "But you only came over to boss us around! You think we can't look after Sooty and Sweep by ourselves."

Mandy shook her head. "Georgia, it's a big responsibility —" This time, she was interrupted by a loud bleat from Sooty. His eyes looked dull and pale.

"You're upsetting our lambs!" cried Georgia, her bottom lip starting to tremble. "I'm going to make them some more milk. That will make them feel better." She turned and ran toward the cowshed.

"No, Georgia!" Mandy called. "Milk isn't the answer to everything. If you'll just read some of these articles —"

"I think you should go home now," Max said crossly.

"Max, we honestly think these lambs are feeling sick," said James. "I know you and Georgia love Sooty and Sweep, but you haven't been shown how to feed them correctly."

"You're just being mean to us!" Max protested.

"This isn't about you," Mandy insisted, trying not to lose her temper. "It's about Sooty and Sweep getting sick, maybe even dying because you aren't feeding them the right things! Do you want that to happen?"

Max blinked, his eyes suddenly watery. "I don't want them to die." He gulped.

Mandy felt a bit bad for scaring him. "Look, there's plenty we can do to help. I'll go and say I'm sorry to your sister first. I know I upset her."

She found Georgia filling a bottle from a bucket of white powder. "Are you all right?" Mandy asked.

"I'm fine," said Georgia, wiping her eyes. "Stop spying on me."

"I'm just trying to look after Sooty and Sweep," Mandy assured her. She peered at the bucket. "Is that ovine milk powder?" Her mom had told her that "ovine" was the technical word for sheep, just like "bovine" referred to cows.

"It's special sheep powder that Great-uncle Sam got for us," Georgia replied, measuring out the amount with a chipped china teacup.

"Didn't it come with a measuring scoop?"

"Max lost it, so now I'm using this," said Georgia.

By now, the clear plastic bottle was more than half-full of powder. "How do you know you're giving them the right amount?" Mandy asked.

Georgia mixed the powder with warm water from a thermos flask. "I've been giving them extra as a treat because they like it so much," she explained.

"But if the milk is too concentrated, and they're not

getting any other food, it could make them sick!" Mandy told her, feeling more and more worried. "Georgia, where's your Great-uncle Sam?"

"Why?" she challenged.

"Because I'm going to ask him to call a vet!" Mandy said firmly.

"He already has," came a grumpy voice behind her.

Sam Western was standing in the doorway of the cowshed.

Mandy stared at him in astonishment. "You have?"

"And I came as soon as I could!" said Dr. Emily, stepping into view just behind him.

"Mom!" Mandy could hardly believe her eyes. "I thought you were busy all day!"

"I am," she said ruefully. "But after what you'd already told me about Sooty and Sweep, I came as soon as Mr. Western called."

"I could see for myself those lambs weren't doing very well when I checked on them this morning," said Mr. Western.

"You *all* think we've made our lambs sick!" said Georgia. She threw down the plastic bottle and burst into tears. "We only wanted to take care of them!"

"Come on, honey, don't cry," Sam Western said awkwardly. To Mandy's surprise, he crouched down and put his hand on the girl's shoulder. "It's my fault for not spending more time with you and Max, and making sure you were feeding them right."

Mandy swapped an incredulous look with her mom. It wasn't often that Sam Western showed his softer side!

"Taking care of animals isn't a game," he went on. Then he seemed to realize Mandy and her mom were staring, and the old gruffness crept back into his tone. "It's a business. And if anything happens to those lambs before the end of next week, Fred Ridings will charge me for them!" He straightened up. "I'd like you to check them over, Dr. Emily, and tell young Georgia exactly how to look after them so I don't have to pay for you to come out here again!"

Emily Hope nodded. "Understood," she said. "Coming, Mandy?"

"I'll be with you in a minute," Mandy said. She crouched down beside Georgia as Sam Western stomped away.

Georgia wouldn't look at her. "You think I'm just a stupid little girl," she muttered.

"No, I don't," Mandy said truthfully. "If no one told you how to look after the lambs, it's not your fault. And if you're willing to learn what Sooty and Sweep really need, then there won't be a better substitute mother than you."

Georgia raised her head, her blue eyes swimming

with tears, and gave Mandy a wobbly smile. "I think I'd like to look at those magazines you brought."

Mandy smiled back. "Come on, then. Let's go and get them from James — and see what we can do to help my mom!"

After Mandy had told her mom about the milk powder, Dr. Emily examined the lambs herself. Sweep bleated plaintively as she pressed his tummy. "I'm afraid Sooty and Sweep are both badly dehydrated," she announced.

"Will they die?" Max croaked, his eyes wide with horror. Mandy felt a pang of guilt about what she'd said earlier.

"No, we've caught it in time," said Dr. Emily. "They just needs lots of fresh water."

"Let's find a bucket, Max," said James, taking the little boy by the arm and leading him away.

"Should I still give them milk?" Georgia asked quietly.

"Yes, but only twice a day," said Dr. Emily. "I'll give you another measuring scoop for the powder."

"Why don't you measure out the correct amount and pour it into your teacup?" Mandy suggested. "Mark where the powder comes up to with a pen, and then you'll have a spare scoop in case you lose the other one."

"And put more water into the powder every day,"

advised Dr. Emily. "After a few days, they'll be getting milk-flavored water, and they'll soon lose interest in the bottle altogether. That will make them eat grown-up food like grain and hay instead."

Georgia sighed. "But where will Max and I get *that* from?"

"I can give you some grain suitable for lambs," said Dr. Emily, "and I'll let your great-uncle know where to get some more."

Just then, James and Max came back with two buckets of water. "One lamb drinking-fountain as requested," James announced.

Mandy watched hopefully as they put the buckets down in the pen. The lambs must be really thirsty, but if they'd only been fed from bottles, would they know how to drink from a bucket? She was disappointed but not entirely surprised when Sooty and Sweep kept on bleating, completely ignoring the water.

"They don't know what to do with the bucket." Dr. Emily sighed.

Mandy nodded. "The important thing right now is to get them to drink. They can learn about buckets later." She took the feed bottles from Georgia and filled them with water. Then she passed one each to Max and Georgia. "Here you go."

Soon the lambs were drinking down the water

greedily. Even though it wasn't milk, they were thirsty enough to appreciate a cool drink of water. Sooty's little tail wagged madly, while Sweep could barely stand still. He looked like he was dancing a jig.

"They love it!" Max said breathlessly.

"They *need* it," said Dr. Emily. "Keep giving them bottles of water, not milk, until they stop drinking, OK?"

The twins nodded solemnly. "Thank you for showing us," said Georgia.

"I'll stop by again on the weekend to see how they're doing," said Dr. Emily. "In the meantime, you need to clear out this soiled bedding and sponge down the lambs' legs and hindquarters. The scouring should stop soon."

"And tonight, we're going to read every word of those magazines," Georgia declared. "We'll make sure Sooty and Sweep are ready to go back to their flock and be grown-up sheep!"

Mandy smiled. "That's good to hear."

"Right," said Dr. Emily. "I'll track down Mr. Western so I can speak to him privately, then I'd better go to my other appointments. Do you need a lift home, Mandy?"

"Thanks, but I think we'll stay here till Grandpa comes to get us," Mandy said, and James nodded. "I want to spend as much time with the lambs as I can before we have to change jobs."

Dr. Emily frowned. "What do you mean?"

"From sheep-girl to cowboy!" Mandy joked. "We're going to help transform the Hart's Leap Ranch horses so they look their best for their big day tomorrow."

"Hope and Hunter, grooms to the stars!" James announced. "That's us!"

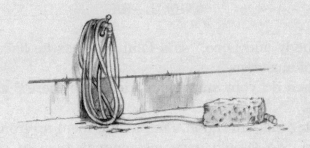

Eight

Grandpa picked up Mandy and James from Upper Welford Hall and drove them back to Animal Ark in time for lunch. No sooner had they cleared the dishes away than Paul arrived in his jeep.

"Hop on board, guys!" he called through the window.

"Where's Lisa?" Mandy asked as she and James climbed in.

"Out in the fields, catching our stars-to-be," Paul replied.

"Who else did Jason Caine choose, besides Fandango and Cougar?" James asked.

"Woody and Loco," said Paul. "I guess he likes the look of mustangs!"

"When do your stunt-rider friends get here?" asked James.

"Later this afternoon. I'm picking them up from the station. We should have just enough time to check where we'll be shooting before it gets dark."

"Where is the shoot taking place?" Mandy asked, as Paul swung the jeep into the graveled drive.

"You know that flat slab of rock out on the west side of the valley, about a half mile away?"

James nodded. "Locals call it the Anvil."

"That's the one," agreed Paul. "It's exactly the right size for the band to stand on and lip-synch the song while we ride around them."

Lisa led Woody into the yard, his hooves ringing loudly on the pavement. "Am I glad to see you guys!" she declared. "These horses have a lot of extra energy today, and it's taken ages to catch these two!"

Woody nudged Mandy, almost knocking her over. "Whoops!" she said, placing her hand against his nose and easing him away.

"He's after a treat," Paul observed.

"I have some pony-nuts in my pocket," said Lisa, holding out a handful of hard pellets. Woody eagerly lipped them off her palm. "A small bribe always makes a horse more cooperative!"

Armed with more pony-nuts, James and Mandy set off to catch the other horses. "Better leave Loco and Fandango to us," said Lisa. "You can bring back Cougar."

"Fantastic!" Mandy grinned.

Cougar was standing on his own at the far side of the field, staring out across the valley. He looked very striking with his black points and buckskin coat framed against the clear blue sky. He glanced around when he heard Mandy and James approach, and stood still as Mandy slipped the halter over his ears.

"No need for the pony-nuts this time," said James, but he offered the mustang a handful, anyway. Cougar turned his head away, not interested.

"He seems a little tucked up," Mandy observed.

"Tucked up in what?" asked James, puzzled.

"I mean he looks thinner, like he's sucking in his flanks. That could mean he's a little dehydrated."

"Not another dehydrated animal!" said James in dismay.

"He can't really be dehydrated, not if he's been eating juicy grass all day. Maybe he's just homesick." Mandy ran her hand along Cougar's mane. "Is that it, boy? Are you missing those Texan plains?"

"Come on, let's get him back to the stables," said James. "Then we can tell Paul and Lisa."

Back in the yard, Lisa had hitched Loco to a rail. Paul was unwinding a long hose, ready to wash him. They looked concerned when Mandy and James came over with Cougar and pointed to his shrunken flank.

"It's not like him to ignore pony-nuts," said Lisa. "But he was fine this morning."

Paul stroked the mustang's face. "Cougar does get into moods from time to time. Maybe he's a little homesick."

"I thought that might be it," Mandy said, relieved.

"Do you want to wash him?" Lisa asked. "He'll probably feel better if you give him a lot of attention."

"Yes, please!" Mandy said eagerly. She hitched Cougar to the rail next to Loco while Paul dragged the hose over. Mandy let the gently running water wash over Cougar's hooves before slowly working her way up his legs. She knew that gave him a chance to get used to the cold water before it touched sensitive areas like his tummy.

James got a sponge and a bottle of horse shampoo, and together they gently scrubbed at Cougar's wheat-colored coat until it was clean and soft. Cougar stood like a rock, his head resting on the taut lead rope. Next to him, Loco sidestepped and swished his tail, flicking soapsuds over Lisa and making Cougar look like the best-behaved horse in the world!

But Mandy still felt worried. Cougar had been really friendly toward her until now, but he didn't seem to be responding to any of her attention, even when she washed areas like his face and neck.

"He trusts you, Mandy," suggested James, catching the concern on her face. "He knows you would never hurt him."

Mandy wished she could believe that was the real reason Cougar was so calm and quiet. But his eyes looked glazed and distant as he stared out over the paddock. "I wish you could tell me how you were feeling, boy," she murmured.

When Cougar's coat had dried in the breeze, they led him into his stall in the barn and helped Lisa wash Woody and Fandango. They were more cooperative than Loco had been under the cold water, but neither of them stood as still as Cougar. Mandy grew more troubled — this wasn't normal behavior for a lively young horse.

As the daylight started to fade, Paul appeared with a large white shopping bag. "I've got to go pick up Frank and Jodie now," he said. "Their train gets into York in a couple of hours."

James sighed. "Does that mean you need to take us back?"

"Afraid so," said Paul. He grinned. "But you two have been such a couple of stars, there's something I want you to have for tomorrow."

Mandy gasped as he pulled out a dusty-blue Stetson with white suede trim and placed it on her head. It was a perfect fit. "Wow!" she said, taking it off so she could study the beautiful craftsmanship. "It's wonderful! It'll even go with my new shirt."

For James, he produced a real cowboy hat, not a costume store imitation. It was made of black felt complete with a silver buckle. "It's so cool!" said James. "Where did you get it?"

"A friend of a friend supplies costumes for movies," Paul explained. "We ordered some props for the shoot, and we thought you deserved something to say thanks for all your help."

"You mean we can keep these forever?" Mandy gazed at the Stetson with pride. "Thank you!"

"Yeah, thanks!" added James, placing his cowboy hat proudly on his head.

Lisa grinned. "They'll look great when you're watching the video shoot!"

"I hope Cougar's feeling better by then," Mandy said fervently.

Paul nodded. "I checked him just now and he doesn't

have a temperature. But we'll put an extra stable rug on him tonight, and see how he does with his evening feed." He smiled. "Want to say good-bye before we go?"

Mandy and James ran into the barn and down the aisle to Cougar's stall. He was standing at the back of the stable and just looked at them when they appeared at the door, without coming over to say hello.

"I hope you feel better tomorrow," Mandy told him. "We'll be back first thing to make sure you look your best for your star performance!"

Cougar turned his head away, and Mandy's heart went out to him. "You won't feel homesick forever," she promised.

Cougar's ears twitched, but he didn't turn back. James gently tugged Mandy's sleeve, and she followed him back into the yard, where Paul was waiting beside the jeep.

"Just imagine," James exclaimed happily as they drove back through the valley, "if we'd never gotten lost coming down from the tor, we'd never have really gotten to know Paul and Lisa or the horses — or the *Cowboys!*"

"I know," Mandy agreed. "Everything worked out perfectly!"

But inside, she couldn't shake the feeling that things were a long way from perfect, especially for Cougar. She said nothing to James, not wanting to spoil his bubbly mood, but she kept picturing Cougar with that faraway look in his eyes. The thought of the magnificent mustang standing in the corner of his stable, lonely and sad, stayed with Mandy all night until finally she fell into a fitful sleep.

Nine

Mandy was woken not by her alarm clock, but by the telephone in the hall. It was just before six. When the phone rang this early, it meant only one thing — someone urgently needed a vet.

As her dad hurried downstairs to answer the call, Mandy's first sleepy thought was that the sick animal might require a house call — in which case her dad might not be able to take her and James to Hart's Leap Ranch for the video shoot. She couldn't let down the Cookes, and she was desperate to see how Cougar was doing. . . .

She got out of bed and ran onto the landing. "Dad? Who called?"

He appeared at the bottom of the stairs, his face grave. "That was Paul Cooke."

Mandy clutched the banister. "What happened?"

"It's Cougar, sweetie," said Dr. Adam. "He hasn't eaten anything overnight, and Paul said he seems to be having difficulty swallowing."

Mandy's legs almost buckled beneath her, and her eyes prickled with tears. "He's homesick, that's all."

Her dad shook his head. "I'm afraid it sounds more serious than that."

Dr. Emily came out onto the landing and gave Mandy a hug. "Are you going over right now, Adam?"

He nodded.

Mandy wiped her eyes. "I'll get dressed."

"I'll pack you some breakfast," said Dr. Emily. "And I'll call James in a little while and tell him what's happened." She smiled at Mandy. "Come on, honey, be brave. We're not miracle workers, but there's every chance your dad will be able to help Cougar."

Mandy sat tensely in the front seat of the Land Rover, dressed in old jeans and a hooded sweatshirt. She had planned to wear her chaps, shirt, and Stetson today, but that didn't seem appropriate now.

"What do you think might be wrong with Cougar, Dad?" she asked.

He gave her knee a gentle pat. "It's hard to say until I've actually examined him."

Mandy gazed miserably through the windshield. "He seemed out of sorts yesterday, but Paul didn't think it was serious. I feel so blind now."

"You mustn't blame yourself, Mandy," he told her. "It's hard to tell what animals are feeling at the best of times. It would be a lot easier to be a human doctor, where your patients can speak to you!"

Lisa was waiting for them outside the farmhouse. She looked tense and pale. "Thank goodness you're here," she said. "We really appreciate you coming out so early."

"No problem," said Dr. Adam. "Let's take a look at the patient."

As Mandy followed Lisa and her dad across the yard, she noticed a man dressed as a cowboy grooming Fandango, who was hitched to the rail. A woman in chaps and a fancy vest was riding Loco around the near paddock, going from halt to canter and back again in just a few strides. Mandy's heart flipped over. They must be Frank and Jodie, the other stunt riders. They were obviously going ahead with the video shoot, even though Cougar was sick. She felt a tiny bubble of hope that

Cougar might not be too ill, and might even be better by the time the film crew arrived.

The bubble burst as soon as she reached Cougar's stall.

He was lying stretched out on the straw, his breath coming in noisy, shallow rasps. Paul had folded back his blanket so Dr. Adam could examine him, and Cougar looked even thinner than the day before, with his ribs jutting out like a grill.

Lisa gestured helplessly toward the horse as Dr. Adam let himself into the stall. "You can see for yourself how bad he looks," she said. Her eyes filled with tears and she had to stop talking. Mandy took Lisa's hand and squeezed it, and Lisa gripped it tightly back.

Cougar didn't move as Dr. Adam knelt down beside him. Paul looked up, one hand resting lightly on Cougar's mane. "His heart sounds regular to me," he reported. "And his temperature seems OK, too." He frowned. "To be honest, I can't think what could make him this ill so quickly but with so few symptoms."

Mandy's dad took his stethoscope out of his black bag. "Is there any discharge from the nose or eyes?"

"None," said Paul.

"And when did he start losing his appetite?"

"He didn't touch his feed last night, or his hay net," said Lisa. "And Mandy said he wasn't interested in any pony-nuts when she brought him in from the paddock. He certainly doesn't want to eat anything this morning."

Mandy joined her dad in the stall and gently stroked Cougar's back. How could this have happened so fast? She wanted to hug him and not let go, but forced herself to stay calm while her dad continued his examination.

"You're right, he's having some trouble swallowing," observed Dr. Adam. "When did he arrive in the country?"

Paul scratched his head. "About a week ago."

"And where has he been grazing?"

"The paddock on the other side of the track, just above the farmhouse," Lisa answered. She frowned. "Do you think he could have eaten something poisonous? The other horses seem fine."

"Actually, that's often the pattern," Dr. Adam said grimly.

Mandy shivered. "Pattern?" she whispered, twisting her fingers into Cougar's mane. "What pattern?

Dr. Adam didn't reply. "How old is Cougar?" he asked Paul.

"He'll be seven in the fall."

"Any sign of colic lately?"

"No, none," said Lisa.

Mandy felt like her stomach was full of knots. Her dad was asking some strange but very precise questions. She knew he had an idea what was wrong with

Cougar, and by the look on his face it was bad news. "Please, Dad, what do you think it is?"

He stood up slowly. "It looks like grass sickness to me."

Lisa looked horrified. "That's serious, isn't it?"

"Very serious," said Dr. Adam. "It's very rare in North America, but more common over here. No one knows exactly what causes it, not even after a century of investigation. Tiny fungal spores on certain areas of grassland are the likeliest suspects, but there's no hard evidence yet. And no certain cure." He let out a deep breath. "I'm really sorry to tell you this, but I'm afraid grass sickness is usually fatal."

"Fatal?" Mandy echoed. The stable spun around her. "Cougar can't die! He hardly looked sick yesterday!"

"The symptoms hit hard and very rapidly," Dr. Adam explained.

"But you don't know for sure it *is* grass sickness, right?" Paul said hopefully.

"I can't run any tests that will tell us for sure without an invasive operation to take a sample from Cougar's gut," said Mr. Hope. "And right now, he's too weak to survive an anesthetic. But the symptoms include loss of appetite, spectacular weight loss, and difficulty swallowing. Research has shown that horses who've been under stress recently are more likely to contract the illness. Cougar's traveled a long way from home, his routine has changed . . ."

Lisa's voice was so choked she could barely get out the words. "Are you saying this is our fault, for bringing Cougar here?"

"No, not at all," Dr. Adam assured her. "It's just a factor that might have left him more vulnerable to whatever causes the disease." He ran his hands through his hair, suddenly looking tired. "There are three types of grass sickness. The acute and subacute forms take hold extremely quickly, and the horse never recovers. Cougar isn't showing the most serious symptoms that would mean he has the chronic form of the illness. That's good news, because it's sometimes treatable. Even so, I should warn you that his chances are less than fifty percent. And if he doesn't improve quickly, we may have to make a tough decision."

Mandy blinked. She knew what her dad meant. "You can't put Cougar down!"

"The paralysis could spread through his gut," said Dr. Adam. "He'd suffer huge amounts of pain, and we can't let that happen. If he doesn't get any better, then putting him to sleep would be the kindest thing to do."

"Well, now you've given us the bad news," said Paul gruffly, "what can we do right now that might help?"

Dr. Adam looked down at the exhausted mustang.

"He'll need around-the-clock care for the next twenty-four hours at least. You need to do everything you can to persuade him to eat because when all is said and done, this is a battle that Cougar has to fight on his own. If he's going to pull through, he's really got to want to live."

"Oh, Cougar," Mandy whispered. "Please don't leave us!"

"I'll put him on a drip to ease the dehydration, but we must get some high-energy food into him, stuff that's easily swallowed," Dr. Adam went on. "Lisa, do you have anything like syrup around?"

"Like molasses, you mean? Sure."

"Chop some vegetables, mix in some oats and soak the whole thing in the molasses," Dr. Adam instructed. "That might tempt him to eat."

"I'll do it right now," said Lisa, wiping her eyes on her sleeve.

"You should keep horses out of the paddock, too, just in case," added Mr. Hope. "The other fields should be OK, but keep an eye on all the horses."

Lisa shook her head wearily. "It's going to be a tough day. The film crew and the band are due to arrive soon."

"Well, you must keep the barn as quiet as you can," said Dr. Adam. "Cougar needs careful nursing, and there should be someone with him at all times."

Lisa nodded and hurried away.

"Of all the days to have a video shoot," groaned Paul.

"I can stay with Cougar," Mandy said at once. "And when James gets here, he'll stay, too, I know he will."

Paul looked doubtful. "I appreciate the offer, Mandy, but it might be better if Lisa or I take responsibility for caring for him."

"Actually, Mandy's a very experienced animal nurse," Dr. Adam put in. "I'm absolutely confident that she could look after Cougar while you're taking care of the shoot, as long as you can check in every couple of hours."

Mandy shot her dad a watery smile to show she was grateful for his support.

"There's nothing technical about the treatment," Dr. Adam went on. "Cougar just needs lots of human contact to keep him awake and willing to fight. He'll also need frequent grooming because his coat will get sweaty and dirty quickly. He'll be more comfortable if he's kept clean and dry."

"I understand," Mandy said solemnly.

Dr. Adam stood up. "Right, let's set up the drip. I don't think Cougar's in a hurry to stand up, so we'll leave him lying in deep straw, and I'll fix the saline bag to the stable wall."

Paul nodded. "I'll get more straw to keep him warm."

"Good idea," said Dr. Adam. "I need to get some saline from the Land Rover, too."

As the two men left the barn, Cougar shifted his head around and looked up at Mandy. His eyes were dull and glazed, but there was a pain and desperation in his expression that tugged at her heart. It was like he was pleading with her to help.

Mandy bent over and rested her face against his cheek. "Dad says you have to fight this battle yourself," she murmured. "But I'm here to fight it with you. We're in this together. I won't leave your side, Cougar, not until you're better. And that's a promise!"

Paul came back with another bale of straw and shook it around Cougar so that he was almost hidden in the clean, deep bedding. Dr. Adam set up the drip, and Mandy noticed Cougar didn't even flinch when the needle was inserted into his neck. Outside, she heard the crunch of heavy tires on gravel and a growl of engines.

Lisa appeared with a basin of finely chopped vegetables in sticky molasses. "Mr. Caine and the Cowboys are here," she reported.

"We'll get to them in a moment," said Paul. He held a handful of vegetables close to Cougar's mouth.

"Please eat it, boy," Mandy urged. "Please."

But Cougar didn't even move his lips.

"It's early yet," Dr. Adam said quietly. "He's feeling confused, distressed, and is in a good deal of pain. But he needs his strength. He must eat soon. Otherwise . . ."

He didn't need to finish the sentence. Mandy could feel tears stinging the backs of her eyes again, and Paul put his arm around Lisa's shoulder.

"I'll stop by later," said Dr. Adam. "I hope the video shoot goes as well as it can under the circumstances." He squeezed Mandy's shoulder. "Bye, sweetie. Keep your chin up."

Mandy nodded, tracing her finger up and down Cougar's nose. "You must get better," she told him. "You *must*."

"Is there any way I can drop out of the video shoot, Paul?" asked Lisa. "I should be here."

"We promised the record company four riders," Paul reminded her gently.

Lisa sighed. "And we could really use the money and the publicity now."

"I know," said Paul. "But we're very lucky — Cougar responds well to Mandy, and she loves him to pieces. I'll go greet the video crew while you saddle up Bobcat. I bet Jason Caine won't even be able to tell the difference between her and Cougar."

"OK." Lisa half-smiled. "Thanks for all you're doing, Mandy."

"Yes, thank you," said Paul. "Between you and your dad, I'm sure this mustang's in the best possible hands."

"I hope so," Mandy murmured as Paul and Lisa left the barn and she and Cougar were left alone. But as she crouched in the straw, stroking Cougar's damp neck, she didn't feel confident about anything.

A few minutes later, Jason Caine stormed into the barn. "Where's this sick horse?" he boomed.

Cougar flinched at the noise and tried to shift in the straw. "Be quiet!" Mandy hissed over the door at Mr. Caine. She tried to calm Cougar before he pulled out his drip. "If you have a question, you need to see Paul."

"He's out there giving Vicki Baker a line of excuses about why we can't use this horse." The director peered into the stall. Mandy thought he'd see a lot better if he removed his dark glasses. "I bet the horse isn't that sick. I know how much you animal lovers exaggerate. Can't you just give him some vitamins or something?"

Mandy stared at him in disbelief. "Look at him!" she gasped. "He's fighting for his life!"

Jason Caine took off his sunglasses. "Oh, *typical*." He threw his arms up in the air in despair. "It would have to be the star of the whole thing, wouldn't it! Useless animal."

Mandy couldn't believe what she was hearing. "Do you think Cougar wanted to get sick?" She fought back tears. "He could die!"

The director raised his eyebrows. "I'm sure you're overdramatizing, dear. Horses are pretty tough."

"Not all the time." Mandy wound her fingers in the mustang's mane. "Please, leave Cougar in peace!"

"You heard her, Jason," came a familiar voice.

Mandy looked up through her tears to see Mitch McFadden standing beside Mr. Caine.

"So, now the heartthrob's telling *me* what to do? That's perfect!" Jason Caine spluttered. "I'm your director, remember?"

"And *that* is a very sick horse who needs rest, support, and love," Mitch said calmly.

"Just what I need." Jason Caine sighed. "A sentimental star! In case you've forgotten, we've got a video to make," Mr. Caine said impatiently.

"This horse needs rest and quiet." Mitch pointed to the barn doors. "So please, will you just leave?"

The director's mouth opened and closed helplessly. Clearly, few people had talked to him like this before. Finally, he turned and stomped out of the horse barn, fuming.

"Sorry about that," Mitch said to Mandy. "Jason's under a lot of pressure to get this video done, but he shouldn't have said what he did. Cougar's bad, isn't he? I heard Paul mention grass sickness."

Mandy nodded, too upset to be starstruck. "He . . . he might not pull through, my dad says."

"When Tigra first hurt her leg, no one knew if she would be able to walk again," Mitch told her. "It's impossible to describe how much fear and pain you can feel on behalf of a horse that you care for. But, you mustn't give up," he said. "Tigra's leg was really bad, and the vets weren't hopeful. But I stayed up with her all night, comforting her, helping her through the pain . . . I forced myself to think positive, right through those long, lonely waiting hours." He came into the stall and knelt down beside Mandy. "We got through it together." He half-smiled. "Fingers crossed, so will you and Cougar."

Mandy smiled at him. "Thanks," she whispered.

Mitch waited with her in silence for some time. Then Vicki Baker, the girl from the record company, appeared in the doorway. She looked shaken. "Mitch, could I have a word with you?"

"Sure," he said. "What's wrong? Did Jason complain about how rude I was?"

"Worse than that," she said. "He just walked out!"

Mitch frowned. "You're kidding!"

Vicki shook her head. "You know how temperamental he is. He stormed into the kitchen, picked a fight with me and Paul, and told us he was leaving — together with his crew and all the gear!"

"That guy's got a screw loose," said Mitch, shaking his head in disbelief.

"I tried to stop him, but he refused to listen. He said he's going back to the city, and wild horses couldn't drag him back." Vicki sighed. "*Definitely* not wild horses!"

Mandy could hear car doors slamming and engines starting up outside. "What about the video?" she asked.

Vicki shrugged. "We'll have to cancel the shoot."

"But we're so booked up with TV spots in the next month, today is the only time we're free before we release the single," said Mitch worriedly. "Can't you find another crew?"

"Not on such short notice," Vicki told him. "Especially not in the wilds of Yorkshire."

"This is my fault, isn't it?" Mandy bowed her head. "If I hadn't gotten so upset with Mr. Caine —"

"No way is this your fault, Mandy," Mitch assured her. "There are dozens of directors out there, but only one Cougar! We'll find a way around this."

"Yes, we will," Vicki agreed, though Mandy could see she was feeling pretty hopeless. "Let's go and talk to Paul about our options."

"Good luck, Mandy," said Mitch, standing up and

patting her on the shoulder. "I'll keep everything crossed for the two of you."

Mandy nodded miserably as they left the stable. It was great that Mitch was being so sympathetic, but it didn't make her feel any better. Not when Cougar might still die. Gently, she lay her head against the mustang's bony ribs and closed her eyes. Cougar didn't even stir, and Mandy's heart ached as she remembered the way he had snuffled her hair while she was putting on his brushing boots.

"You have to get better, Cougar," she breathed. "Please, boy. You *have to*."

Ten

"He's just the same," Mandy told Paul and Lisa when they came into the barn a half hour later. "He still won't eat."

"Well, at least it'll be quiet around here now," said Paul. "Everyone's gone except Frank and Jodie. They said they'd help look after the other horses today."

"I was crazy to bring us all the way over here," murmured Lisa, crouching down beside Mandy and stroking Cougar's flank. "If we'd stayed in Texas, none of this would have happened. I should never have forced you to come, Paul."

"Hey, you didn't exactly twist my arm," Paul reminded

her. "This was a great opportunity. We sent all our horses over the best possible route and in the most comfort possible. We can't blame ourselves for Cougar's sickness."

Talking about the horses' transportation reminded Mandy that Paul and Lisa were desperately trying to set up a business. "Will you still get paid, even though the shoot's been canceled?" she asked awkwardly.

Paul shrugged. "Vicki talked about a cancelation fee, but it's far less than we planned for, and losing the free publicity hurts, too." He put his arm around Lisa's shoulders. "But we'll survive. I just hope Cougar does, too."

"I'll get a grooming kit," Mandy decided. "I haven't brushed him yet."

"Why not take five minutes to grab some breakfast?" Paul suggested. "You haven't moved for almost three hours."

Mandy felt a bit light-headed as she stood up. "Maybe you're right. Just for a few minutes."

Outside, the sunlight was painfully bright. The horses had been turned out into the safe paddocks, and the yard was silent. Mandy walked like a zombie toward the farmhouse. She'd just come through the back door when the doorbell rang.

She rushed to answer it, hoping Jason Caine had come back to make the video after all.

But it was James, wearing his cowboy outfit. "My mom gave me a ride over as soon as she could," he said. "I thought there would be trailers and things everywhere. . . . What's going on? Is Cougar all right?"

"Oh, James," Mandy gasped. "*Nothing's* all right!"

Mandy told James everything. He stared at her as he listened, his face a mixture of horror and disbelief. When she had finished, he insisted on going straight to the barn to see Cougar. Mandy grabbed some fruit and a couple of muffins from the kitchen before following him outside. Then, together with Paul and Lisa, they began a long, desperate vigil for Cougar.

The day crawled by as they took turns caring for him. Every couple of hours, Mandy carefully brushed Cougar's coat to keep him comfortable. Lisa presented him with every one of his favorite foods — apples, carrots, even a roll of mints — but he wasn't interested in eating anything.

"I made us some lunch," James announced a little after two o'clock. "Just sandwiches, I'm afraid." The four of them munched in silence, sitting side by side in Cougar's stall. Mandy couldn't taste a thing.

As afternoon gave way to evening, Cougar was too weak to swish his tail at the flies that buzzed around his back so Mandy tried to keep them away for him. Lisa had applied some fly repellent, but Cougar was sweating so much that the fine powder came off even with the most gentle grooming.

"We're here for you, Cougar," Mandy kept saying again and again. "You're going to get better. You *are*." She felt that if only she could wish strongly enough, the mustang's condition would improve. It *had* to.

Mandy's mom called twice during the day, and at six o'clock Dr. Adam arrived at the ranch in person to check on the patient — and on Mandy.

"How are you feeling?" he asked, kissing her on her forehead.

"Never mind me," Mandy insisted. "I think Cougar's looking better, don't you?"

Dr. Adam shot her a sideways look. "Has he eaten anything?"

Mandy looked desperately at Lisa. "Um, kind of . . . He licked my finger once."

"The truth is, Adam, he hasn't touched anything all day," said Lisa flatly.

Dr. Adam nodded. He listened to Cougar's chest, took his temperature, and studied his eyes. "Well, there's no change since this morning," he reported. "But at least that means he's not getting worse." He gently pinched some of Cougar's skin, then let it go. "The elasticity of his skin is good, so he's not dehydrated. But he can't keep fighting without solid fuel. He *has* *to* find his appetite."

"We won't give up," Mandy promised. "We'll keep trying."

"You look like you could use some rest, honey," said her dad. "Maybe you and James should leave Paul and Lisa to —"

"No, Dad!" Mandy pleaded. "I want to stay." She turned to Paul and Lisa. "Please?"

"Of course you can stay," said Lisa. "If it's OK with your dad."

"She's no trouble, Adam," Paul added.

Dr. Adam smiled. "All right. But try to get some sleep, Mandy. I'll come back first thing tomorrow."

James cleared his throat. "I'd better go back with your dad, Mandy. Mom's expecting me for dinner. But can I come again with you tomorrow, Dr. Adam?"

"Of course," he said, and gestured for James to lead the way out of the stable. He paused at the door and looked back. "Good luck, everyone."

Through the window in the back of the stall, Mandy watched the sky grow dark. When Lisa had told Paul she was going to spend the night out in the stall with Cougar, Mandy had insisted on staying there, too. It was freezing cold, but Paul supplied pillows and warm blankets, and visited regularly with hot water bottles and cocoa to help them through the night.

Mandy dozed, but only for a few minutes at a time. She kept trying to feed Cougar the molasses mixture, but he just stared straight ahead, not responding. Outside, the clouds cleared away, revealing a handful of stars in the night sky. Mandy wished on every one that Cougar would soon recover. But she knew that with every hour that passed, his chances grew slimmer.

Usually when Mandy stayed up with a sick animal, the hours seemed to crawl past. But this time it seemed like only a few moments before the sky began to lighten with the first pink streaks of sunrise. If her dad arrived and saw no improvement . . .

"Please, Cougar," she whispered, trying not to wake Lisa. "I know I've been nagging you all night, but you *have* to eat." She pressed some sticky oats and chunks of apple to his lips, feeling the warmth of his breath on her fingers but nothing else.

"Oh, Cougar." She slumped forward, too tired even to cry.

Suddenly, her sleepy eyes snapped open. The mustang's lips were fumbling against her hand, stirring the oats on her palm.

"Cougar?" She lifted her head slowly so as not to

startle him. Cougar blinked, but lipped up some more of the oats.

"Lisa, wake up!" she whispered. "Cougar's trying to eat!"

Lisa sat up, instantly alert. "You're right! Try some more!"

Mandy grabbed another handful of oats, but this time Cougar didn't move when she held them close to his mouth.

"At least he had a little!" Lisa jumped up as if she'd spent the night in the most comfortable bed in the world. "I'm going to tell Paul."

They came back a few minutes later. Paul was still wearing his pajamas and shivering in the crisp dawn. Mandy offered Cougar some chunks of apple — and this time he crunched them up, still without lifting his head off the straw but definitely showing signs of a returning appetite.

"You fabulous, fabulous boy!" Paul whispered, crouching down to ruffle Cougar's mane. He looked up at Mandy and grinned. "You're a great nurse!"

Dr. Adam arrived with James a couple of hours later, at eight-thirty. Paul showed him through to the stable, and Mandy saw they were all wearing a look of cautious optimism.

"Paul told me the news," said Dr. Adam. "If Cougar's started trying to eat, that's an encouraging sign."

"Does it mean he's going to be all right?" James asked eagerly.

"He's still very ill," Dr. Adam warned. "He has a long way to go."

"He's going to make it," Mandy insisted. "I just know he is."

"Why don't you and Lisa get some sleep away from all this straw?" said Paul. "Frank and Jodie can help me with the morning routine."

"I'll help, too," said James.

Mandy yawned. "I suppose I am a little tired."

"A little?" Mandy's dad smiled. "A bell boy could carry those bags under your eyes!"

"I'm sure Jodie won't mind you using her bed in the guest room," said Lisa.

"Oh, and your mom packed you a change of clothes," said Dr. Adam, passing Mandy a backpack. "Paul, James, keep trying to feed Cougar. I'll drop in again at lunchtime for a progress report. See you then."

Mandy slept well in the comfy guest room and woke up around twelve, feeling much more rested. She looked out on to the landing and saw Lisa passing in a fluffy white robe.

"How's Cougar?" Mandy asked nervously.

"The boys say he's doing fine," Lisa told her. "Would you like to take a bath? There's plenty of hot water."

"Yes, please," Mandy said. The mountain of bubbles looked tempting after she had filled the bath, but she didn't linger too long, as she was eager to see how Cougar was improving. As soon as she had put on clean clothes, she hurried downstairs.

She had just reached the kitchen when the phone rang. "Could you get that for me?" Lisa called from the living room.

Mandy picked up the phone. "Hart's Leap Ranch."

"This is Mitch McFadden. Just calling to see how Cougar is doing."

"It's Mandy," she said. "Cougar started eating!"

"Fantastic!" said Mitch. "I'd love to visit but we're in Manchester right now, promoting the new single."

"Is there really no chance you can shoot your video here?" Mandy asked.

"Vicki's been working on it, but I think we'll have to shoot something back in London," said Mitch. "We only have one free day due to a cancelation, and that's Wednesday. There's not enough time to get a new video crew up there." He paused as someone spoke to him in the background. "Sorry, I have to go. But I'm keeping Cougar in my thoughts, OK? Give my best to everyone."

"I will, Mitch," Mandy told him. "Bye."

She was just replacing the receiver when James came into the kitchen. "Who were you talking to?" he asked.

"Mitch McFadden," she replied airily.

James's jaw dropped. "No way! That's so cool!"

Mandy smiled. "I suppose it is. I don't really think of him as a pop star now — he's just wild about horses, like we are. How's Cougar?"

"He's still lying down. Your dad is with him." James sounded concerned, and Mandy felt a tremor of worry as she hurried out to the barn.

She knew horses weren't designed to lie down for long periods because it put too much pressure on their lungs and internal organs. That's why they were able to sleep standing up, plus it meant they could run away quickly if they were threatened by a predator. Cougar had to find the strength to stand up before he started having breathing problems.

She found her dad talking with Paul outside the mustang's stall. "Cougar *is* going to make it, isn't he?" she burst out.

"I hope so, Mandy," said Dr. Adam. "It's great that he managed to eat, but until he's back on his feet, he hasn't turned the corner. I've removed the drip because he's not dehydrated anymore, but I can't do anything to get him standing up."

Mandy looked into the stall. To her dismay, Cougar looked no better than when she'd left him that morning. She let herself into the stable and went over to kneel down beside him.

"I know you're worn out," she whispered. "But you have to stand up! It will help you get better."

She straightened up to remove a prickle of straw from her arm, and saw Cougar following her moment with his eyes. She was sure they were more open than before. There was even a slight gleam in them, as if he were genuinely curious about what she was doing.

She got an idea then. Slowly, keeping eye contact, Mandy started to get to her feet. Cougar raised his head a little higher to keep her in view. She didn't dare blink in case he looked away. "Come on, Cougar. You can do it," she whispered.

She stood up and backed away, still clinging to Cougar's gaze with her eyes.

Cougar tossed his head and snorted. Then, clumsily and with his eyes rolling, he propped his forelegs up in the straw. He paused for a long enough moment for Mandy to fear she'd lost him again. But then — he heaved himself up to his feet. He stood for a moment with his legs braced, arching his neck in a long stretch. Then he shook himself and looked at Mandy with his ears pricked, as if he knew he'd done something amazing.

Mandy gasped. "You did it!"

"The two of you did it," Paul corrected her, stepping into the stall. "That was incredible, Mandy!"

James's head then appeared over the stall door. "He's standing up!"

"Yup!" said Mandy. "I noticed him watching me, and when I moved away, he decided he didn't want to be lying down anymore."

Dr. Adam came in with his stethoscope to check Cougar's heart rate. "You obviously built quite a bond with him last night."

"I think that there was a connection from the moment they met," Paul declared.

Mandy was too happy to speak. She put her arms around Cougar's neck and pressed her face into his coat.

"Well, he's got a long, slow recovery ahead of him, but I'd say he's out of immediate danger," said Dr. Adam. "That's what makes grass sickness such a problem for vets — we have to rely on the horse fighting its own way out of trouble. Cougar will find eating and drinking a lot easier now that he's standing up, so I'll give you some powders that dissolve in water to help restore his strength."

Paul nodded. "Whatever you say, Doc!"

Mandy pulled away from Cougar. "Has Cougar really won his battle, Dad?"

"You fought it together," Dr. Adam told her. "And you both won."

Less than an hour later, Cougar started pulling at his hay net, slowly but determinedly. Mandy felt as proud of him as if he'd just won a major competition.

"Clever boy!" she told him, patting his neck. Suddenly, a wave of exhaustion hit her, and she staggered.

Lisa caught her by the arm. "Now that you've worked your magic on this fellow, how about going home for a real rest?"

Mandy had to admit the thought of sleeping in her own bed was very tempting. "Do you promise to call if he gets worse again?"

"I promise."

Mandy nearly dozed off in the car as Paul gave her and James a lift back to Welford. She felt like she hadn't seen her bedroom in days and was soon asleep.

James called her that night to see how she was feeling. Mandy had just come downstairs for dinner. Her mom let her take the call while she was waiting for her soup to heat.

"Mom says she'll take us to see Cougar again tomorrow," Mandy told James. "We can see how Sooty and Sweep are doing on our way."

"I'd almost forgotten about the lambs!" James admitted. "I hope they're doing better."

"Me, too," Mandy said with feeling. "But I'm sure Georgia and Max have been doing a great job." With Cougar standing up and eating, she suddenly felt as though everything would be all right!

Mandy and James set off with Dr. Emily right after breakfast. "You've got two house calls to make this morning," she declared. "You're like a couple of vets!"

"I'm a very forgetful one," Mandy confessed. "I completely forgot that it's Easter! And I haven't given out my candy."

"Neither have I," James realized.

"Don't worry," said Dr. Emily. "We can hand them out later. It'll taste even better once we know how Cougar and the lambs are doing."

The sun shone warmly on the cobblestones as Mandy and James headed across the yard to the converted sty. A familiar bleating noise greeted them.

"Looks like Sooty and Sweep are up," said James. "They're real Easter lambs!"

Mandy reached the pen first and leaned over the wall. Two bouncing bundles of gray-and-black fluff scampered over to nibble at her fingers.

"They're so much better!" she exclaimed. Gently

extracting her fingers, she let herself into the pen for a closer look. She rubbed Sooty's soft little sides, and felt Sweep's bony head butting against the backs of her knees. Mandy turned to pet him, and as she did so, Sooty trotted over to the bucket of water in the corner and started drinking.

"Who's a smart little lamb?" James smiled. "Sorry, *lambs*," he corrected himself as Sweep went over to drink with Sooty at the bucket.

Dr. Emily joined Mandy in the pen. "There's no sign of scouring," she confirmed, "and they're looking a lot less bloated. Let's try this." She pulled a pear from her pocket, gouged out a chunk with her thumbnail, and offered it to the lambs. Sooty scampered over and nibbled it straight off her palm.

"You certainly know what to do with solid food now, don't you?" Mandy laughed. She grinned at James. "Georgia and Max obviously took those tips to heart!"

Sweep bleated plaintively for his own piece of pear, so Dr. Emily let Mandy feed him some. His lips tickled her hand, and he blinked up at her with dark eyes while he munched.

"I'd say these lambs are back on track for a successful weaning by the end of the week," Dr. Emily declared. "Let's go and congratulate Max and Georgia!"

They knocked on the door of the farmhouse, and Sam

Western greeted them. While Dr. Emily talked with him about the lambs, Mandy and James went through to the TV room where the twins were eating chocolate Easter eggs while watching a cartoon.

"Mandy and James!" cried Georgia. "We weren't expecting you!"

"We just thought we'd pop in and say hi," Mandy explained. "Sooty and Sweep seem to be doing really well."

Max nodded. "Those articles you gave us were the best!"

"I really *am* an expert on raising lambs now," Georgia said proudly. "I want to do it for a living when I grow up!"

Mandy smiled. "I'm not sure how many professional lamb raisers there are," she admitted, "but maybe you'll start a new trend!"

"Hold on a minute," said Georgia, excitedly checking her watch as the cartoon reached a cliff-hanger. "It's time for the commercials!"

"It can't be a very good cartoon if they'd rather watch the commercials!" Mandy whispered to James.

Max and Georgia put down their chocolate eggs and knelt in front of the screen. James started to say something, but Max shushed him. "Mom's new commercial is on!" he explained.

Mandy felt impressed. "I didn't know your mom was an actress."

"She's not *in* the commercial, she *made* it!" Georgia corrected her. "Well, her company did, anyway."

"This is it!" cried Max. "Shhhh!"

On the TV screen, a group of well-groomed boys and girls zoomed toward the camera on in-line skates, accompanied by some cool pop music and special effects. First they were skating on a sidewalk, then on water, then inside a computer game. The action kept cutting, faster and faster in time with the music, before a voice-over announced the name of the skate brand, and the kids took off into the sky. When it had finished, Georgia and Max cheered and clapped.

"That was awesome!" declared Max.

"I think it's Mom's best commercial yet."

"It *was* good," Mandy agreed. "Almost like —" She trailed off, staring at James. "Almost like a music video!"

James gasped. "Are you thinking what I'm thinking? If Vicki Baker can't find a music video crew available on the Cowboys' last free day . . ."

"Maybe they could try a crew who make commercials!" Mandy finished. "It's got to be worth a try!"

James turned back to the twins. "Is your mom still in York?"

"On Easter Sunday? Don't be silly!" Georgia shook her head. "She's here, spending the day with us!"

"Quick, James — let's ask my mom to talk to the twins' mom and find out if she can help!"

She ran into the kitchen to find a tall woman with short dark hair and stylish eyeglasses had joined Dr. Emily and Sam Western.

Mandy's mom frowned. "Is there something wrong, Mandy? This is Sam's niece — and the twins' mother — Fenella Hammond."

Mrs. Hammond smiled. "Georgia and Max have told me so much about you and James. I'm very glad to meet you."

"Not as glad as we are to meet you!" Mandy assured her.

James popped up behind Mandy. "There's something we need to ask you, Mrs. Hammond."

Dr. Emily looked at them with a puzzled expression. "Is everything all right?"

"That depends on Mrs. Hammond," Mandy explained, crossing her fingers. "If she can help us by coming to the rescue of the Cookes and the Cowboys, then *everything* will be all right!"

Eleven

"Come on, Dad!" Mandy shouted up the stairs the following Wednesday. "We don't want to be late for the video shoot!"

"All right! I'll be with you in a minute," came the reply.

"Yes, come on, Adam," teased Dr. Emily. "If Fenella Hammond can assemble a full video crew in Yorkshire in three days flat, you should to be able to transport Mandy and James to Hart's Leap Ranch before lunchtime!"

Mandy laughed. It was a glorious morning, and she

was fizzing with excitement. She couldn't believe how well everything had worked out.

On Sunday, at Upper Welford Hall, Fenella Hammond had listened carefully to the tale of how the Cowboys had lost their video director. Mandy's dreams started to come true when it turned out that making music videos was something Mrs. Hammond had always wanted to try out. Paul and Lisa were pretty thrilled when they heard, too! They put her in touch with Vicki Baker, and preparations got under way at once for a shoot on Wednesday.

"You don't think it's all a bit too good to be true, Mom, do you?" Mandy wondered. "The Cowboys will get to make the video they really wanted, Paul and Lisa will get publicity for their business, and Mrs. Hammond could end up making lots more music videos. And best of all, Cougar's really getting better."

"Of course it's not too good to be true," said her mom. "The Cookes deserve it."

Dr. Adam rushed down the stairs. "We just have to get James and we're on our way!"

James was waiting outside his house. He was wearing his cowboy outfit, topped off with the hat Paul and Lisa had given him.

"You two look terrific, I must say," said Dr. Adam.

"You should ask Mitch McFadden if he's auditioning two more Cowboys!"

Mandy smiled, feeling glad she'd put on her new shirt, her leather chaps, and her Stetson. "I'm happy just to watch the video being made."

"It's been an Easter to remember all right," said James. "No one at school will believe what we've done this spring break!"

The ranch was a bustle of activity, and Dr. Adam had to squeeze the Land Rover into a tiny gap beside an enormous white trailer. Two women staggered past with an assortment of rodeo-style costumes. A man carrying a curling iron and a makeup brush nodded to them as he went inside the trailer. Three more men were tinkering with a lighting rig in the back of a van.

Vicki Baker was speaking with Fenella Hammond by the front door of the farmhouse. She broke off to wave to Mandy and James. "Glad you could all make it," she said. "Thanks so much for putting me in touch with Fenella. What a find!"

"Glad to be of service," said Mrs. Hammond, winking at Mandy.

The door opened and Max appeared. "Look, Georgia, it's Mandy and James!" he called over his shoulder. He stared at their outfits, impressed. "Wow, they really *are* cowboys!"

"How many times do I have to tell you, Max?" complained Georgia, following him out. "They're not —" She stopped when she saw Mandy's chaps and Stetson. "Well, maybe they are!"

Mandy laughed. "Where are the *real* Cowboys?"

"Most of them are getting ready in the trailer," said Vicki. "But Mitch is in the stable, visiting the sick horse."

"Cougar!" Mandy gasped. "I can't wait to see how he's doing."

"Neither can I," said Dr. Adam.

"Go on in," said Vicki. "I'll call you when we're ready to start shooting."

While Dr. Emily continued talking to Mrs. Hammond, Mandy, her dad, and James headed for the barn. Mitch was just coming out with Paul and Lisa. When he saw Mandy and James, he did a double take.

"You two look more authentic than *we* do!" he said.

Lisa grinned. "Howdy, folks. Good to see you all."

"Cougar's doing so much better now," said Paul. "We really want to thank you for all you did for him."

Dr. Adam smiled. "I'm glad it worked out."

"Me, too," Mitch declared. "I could tell Mandy was never going to let that mustang stop fighting." He winked at her. "Positive thinking, right?"

Mandy grinned. "Definitely."

Mitch looked thoughtful. "You know, that really is a cool outfit, Mandy. Yours is great, too, James." He glanced at Paul and Lisa. "I don't suppose you could fix us up with another couple of horses, could you?"

Lisa frowned. "I guess so. Why?"

Mitch turned to Vicki. "You remember we were talking about that scene in the mists to go with the second chorus?"

Vicki nodded as if she knew exactly what he was going to say. "We wanted to hire some extras but the budget didn't stretch to it. However, since Mandy and James look the part already . . ."

James gulped. "You mean — you want me and Mandy in your video?"

"You'd only be in the background," Mitch said apologetically. "But you'd really be helping us out."

"Of course, we'd need written permission from your parents," added Vicki, smiling at Dr. Adam. "And we might want to film an interview with you afterward, asking how it feels to appear in a Cowboys video."

"I know how it feels just to be *asked*." Mandy beamed. "Thanks, Mitch!"

"I'm sure my mom and dad will agree," said James. "Can I ride Fig again, Lisa?"

"No problem," she said. "And since Bobcat's standing

in for Cougar, Mandy, how would you like to ride Chase?"

Mandy pictured the beautiful chestnut horse with the four white socks. He wasn't as special to her as Cougar, but he looked like a great ride. "I'd love to!"

Paul grinned at his wife. "Looks like we'd better go and get them saddled up."

"I'll take care of the paperwork," said Vicki. "Dr. Hope, may I have your signature on the permission form?"

"Gladly," he said. "Then I'll call James's mom before I check in on Cougar."

Mandy looked at James. "Let's go and see him before we have to start the shoot."

Cougar was standing at the back of his stall, but this time he looked around eagerly when Mandy reached his door. He still looked very thin, but he was munching on some feed in his manger and his hay net hung loosely from the metal ring, showing that he'd nearly eaten all the hay. There was a shine to his coat and in his eyes that Mandy hadn't seen for days.

As she slipped into the stable, Cougar walked forward and rested his head gently on her shoulder. Mandy stretched her arms around his neck as far as they would reach and breathed in his delicious warm smell. They'd been on a terrifying journey together on that dark night,

but he'd pulled through — and she'd fought for him **every step** of the way, by loving him and wishing for him to get better.

"He looks so much better!" James exclaimed, coming over to pat Cougar's neck. "He's one tough mustang."

Mandy nodded. Happy tears stung her eyes as she stroked the side of Cougar's face. "Chase is a lovely horse, but I wish I were riding you instead," she whispered. She kissed his nose, and he snuffled softly. "I promise I'll come back and tell you all about the shoot."

"I'm sure there will be other videos," said James. "And Cougar will be the star of every one!"

"Whatever happens," Mandy vowed, leaning her head against Cougar's mane, "he'll always be a star to me."

A couple of hours later, Mandy and James were cantering in the fields with Paul, Lisa, and the two stunt riders, Frank and Jodie. Ahead of them, they could see the large slab of rock known as the Anvil. Vans and trailers were parked on one side of it, and busy huddles of people stood around setting up cameras and lights and loudspeakers. A large machine pumped out special stage smoke that hung eerily around the rock, lending an air of real mystery to the moors.

"Typical, isn't it?" said James. "There's never a good Yorkshire mist when you need it!"

Mandy thought back to the first time she'd seen Cougar, appearing out of the mist like something in a dream. She'd never have guessed in a million years that she'd go for a hike to the tor and find a real American mustang! Now she couldn't imagine *not* having Cougar in her life. She would make sure she was a regular visitor to Hart's Leap Ranch.

Jodie rode up alongside her and patted Woody's neck. "The horses will look fantastic, parading through that!"

"They sure will," Paul agreed, joining them on Loco. He was wearing his black cowboy outfit again, looking exotic and strange against the purple heather in the field.

Lisa cantered up, her face flushed under the brim of her hat. "Let's go prove just how great we can look, OK?"

"Yee-hah!" cried Frank, one hand pulling on Fandango's reins, and the other holding his Stetson high in the air as the bright chestnut pony reared up. They set off at a fast gallop, and Paul and Jodie raced after him with a cheer.

Lisa smiled at Mandy and James. "Don't worry about keeping up. We'll all get into the video, even if we're not going all out. Just go at your own pace."

Suddenly, the Cowboys' new song, "Riding a Storm," burst from the speakers, sounding tinny and quiet as it carried across the moor.

"Guys, they're playing our song!" Lisa declared. "Are you ready to go?"

"You bet!" cried James. He shortened his reins and kicked Fig into a canter.

Mandy paused for a moment, keeping hold of Chase as he pawed restlessly at the ground, and looked back at Hart's Leap Ranch, the buildings looking like toys nestled in the valley. She raised her hat in a silent salute to Cougar. She knew it wouldn't be long before the mustang was running wild and free again.

And then, with a cowboy-style shout of joy, she galloped after Lisa and James, her ears ringing with the sound of Chase's hooves pounding over the turf.